"We got off to a [...]
Rachel acknowledged.

"You don't like me—that's your privilege," she continued. "But surely, out of feeling for a fellow human being, you could do something for me."

Flynn smiled lazily, the first sign that he even recognized the fact that she was speaking. "I used to be human," he muttered, "but luckily I got over it."

"If you can't help me, could you at least recommend someone who can?"

"I'm afraid you're out of luck. You'd better go back home."

"But you don't under—"

"Go home, lady," he said abruptly. "I can't help you."

When she didn't move, he ran his gaze over her body in a blatant insult. "But if you're going to to stay in my room, you'd better get into my bed."

Dear Reader,

Spellbinders! That's what we're striving for. The editors at Silhouette are determined to capture your imagination and win your heart with every single book we publish. Each month, six Special Editions are chosen with *you* in mind.

Our authors are our inspiration. Writers such as Nora Roberts, Tracy Sinclair, Kathleen Eagle, Carole Halston and Linda Howard—to name but a few—are masters at creating endearing characters and heartrending love stories. Their characters are everyday people—just like you and me—whose lives have been touched by love, whose dreams and desires suddenly come true!

So find a cozy, quiet place to read, and create your own special moment with a Silhouette Special Edition.

Sincerely,

The Editors
SILHOUETTE BOOKS

BILLIE GREEN
Voyage of the Nightingale

Silhouette Special Edition

Published by Silhouette Books New York

America's Publisher of Contemporary Romance

SILHOUETTE BOOKS
300 East 42nd St., New York, N.Y. 10017

ISBN: 0-373-09379-9

First Silhouette Books printing May 1987

America's Publisher of Contemporary Romance

Printed in the U.S.A.

Books by Billie Green

Silhouette Special Edition

Jesse's Girl #297
A Special Man #346
Voyage of the Nightingale #379

BILLIE GREEN's

college professor once told her that she was a *natural* writer. But her readers and editors find it hard to believe that she writes one good story after another only because she comes by them naturally. Maybe someday this devoted wife, mother of three and romance writer extraordinaire will create a heroine who is a writer. Then, possibly, we will get a hint of her trials and tribulations.

AUTHOR'S NOTE

While Atuona, on the island of Hiva Oa, is very real and is indeed the capital of the beautiful Marquesas Islands, Pigalle, with its cast of lively characters, exists only in my imagination and has no basis in fact. The Alexandra Islands are entirely fictional.

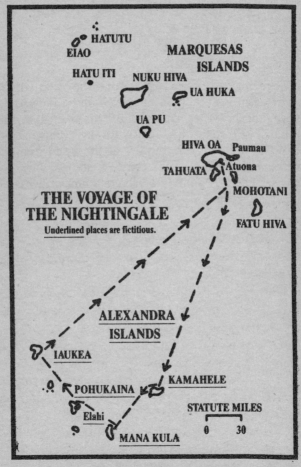

Chapter One

March

Something's wrong here, Jack," Rachel said, riffling through page after page of blueprints. "The whole north end has been changed."

Her gaze drifted out over the open fields as though she could see clearly the shopping complex they wouldn't break ground on for another year. "You see?" she said, nodding toward the fields. "The ice rink should be there, not here at the north end."

The man beside her stared out across the expanse of grass, trying to capture her vision, but his eyes kept straying back to her face.

"It was Mr. Asa's idea, ma'am," he said awkwardly. "I thought he had talked to you about it."

He hid a grin when he heard the muttered profanity. The vulgar word was soft and concise. And, in a flight of fancy uncharacteristic of him, he thought it sounded more like a blessing than a curse. Jack had been around the McNaughts—father and daughter— long enough to know the tolerant affection that colored even their most violent arguments.

A whirring noise that had seemed a part of the Massachusetts wind grew closer and louder. Then suddenly Rachel's linen sailor suit was plastered against her slender body. Her golden blond hair whipped free from a turquoise silk scarf and blew wildly about her face in a joyous emancipation celebration as a helicopter landed not fifty feet away from them.

A young man hopped out of the glass bubble. He bent low in acknowledgment of the spinning blades as he ran toward the two people in the field.

"Asa wants to see you right away, Miss Rachel," he shouted above the noise.

She stared at him for a moment. "Thank you, Ralph."

Rachel's expression gave no clue to the way her pulse raced in anxiety as she handed the bound blueprints to Jack. "You can take these back to the office for me, Jack. We'll try it again next week...after I talk to my dear father."

Damn you, Asa, she thought on the helicopter ride to her father's home. You'd better be all right.

Why did he have to scare her like this? It would most likely be something frivolous—a new jet he had decided to buy, or a deal that had put him one up on all his friends. But lately it had occurred to Rachel that Asa would not always be there. The thought frightened her.

Rachel and her father had never been messy with their emotions. She loved him deeply, but she had had his number for a long time. Asa was a manipulator. It was only in the past five years that he had discovered Rachel would not be manipulated.

But that didn't keep him from trying, she thought with a smile.

Thirty minutes later she walked into her father's walnut-lined study. In an almost undetectable movement she examined his face carefully. It was strong and handsome and, thank God, healthy. Finding nothing amiss, she threw herself into the suede chair across the desk from him.

"What's up?" she asked, her voice slightly impatient.

"I'm fine, daughter," he said sarcastically. "And how are you?"

"Cut the bull, Asa. You didn't send for me so we could chitchat." She sat up straighter. "But while I'm here, maybe you can tell me why on earth you had Rider change the blueprints. That complex is *mine*, Asa. You keep your hands off it."

"Forget the complex—"

"I will not have you meddling—"

"I'm getting married."

She closed her mouth abruptly, her eyes widening. After a moment she said warily, "Sabrina?"

"Hell, no!" The words were explosive. "Where've you been? I haven't seen her in months. It's Paulette."

Rachel relaxed visibly. Her father was not only very wealthy, he was very attractive. Of the two characteristics, it was the wealth that attracted women like Sabrina. Rachel had only met Paulette twice, but she had seen nothing in the woman to worry her.

"Okay," she said, shrugging casually. "You have my blessing. How does Paulette feel about being number six?"

"You mean five."

She shook her head. "Six."

Asa held up one strong, heavily veined hand. "Your mother, Doris, Joan, and Marishna—" he said the name in the heavy Russian accent he always used when he spoke of Mari "—four. Which will make Paulette number five."

"You forgot Thelma."

He frowned, and the lines that formed in his face gave the only clue to his age. "Thelma . . . she was the only one who didn't cost me a fortune. But hell, we were only married for six weeks. Not long enough to even count."

"Poor Thelma," Rachel said, her smile wry. "If she had known that sticking it to you would have kept her in your memory she probably would have developed a little greed."

"I didn't bring you here to talk about Thelma." He shifted in irritation. "I want you to help me plan the wedding."

She stared at him silently. Asa had never asked for her help before. What was he up to? "When is it?"

He leaned forward, shifting some papers. "We thought the middle of July would be nice." His laugh was just a shade too hearty. "No sense waiting at my age."

Silence fell in the room. Asa's hand tightened on a gold pen as though he sensed her unwavering gaze.

"It won't work, Asa," she said at last.

"Well, hell, girl, give it a chance," he said, still avoiding her gaze. "I haven't even married her yet."

She stood and moved to the other side of the desk. Leaning down, she put her arms around his neck and hugged him. "You know what I mean," she said gently. "If you want to get married, then do it, but do it some other time. For more than ten years I've spent every July in the same way. This year will be no different. Don't make me choose between you and Cleve."

"I don't know what the hell you're talking about," he said, his voice blustery. "Can't I arrange a simple little wedding without you accusing me of ulterior motives?"

When she simply stared at him, one brow raised, he shrugged her arms off his neck in irritation. "Why, Rach? Why do you keep wasting your time on your mother's bastard?"

"Don't call him that, Asa," she said, a warning evident in her tone. "They were married before Cleve was born. And now that they're gone, I'm all Cleve has."

"You're all I have, too. But I don't suppose that counts."

She laughed suddenly, her mood lightening at his little boy pose. "Don't try that one on me. You never have fewer than three women on your string at a time." When he opened his mouth to object she said, "And don't try to tell me they're all after your money. For some crazy reason most of them think you need taking care of."

"I do," he said grumpily. "My only child chooses to neglect me, so I have to turn to strangers for affection."

"Now I suppose you're going to try to make me believe that Sabrina with the Mae West breasts was a substitute for me."

For a moment he looked as though he would try just that, then he laughed. "You're too smart for your own good." Leaning back, his face became serious as he threw all pretense aside. "You'll never find him, Rach. Damn it all, he's off in nowhere's backyard. You don't even know which of those confounded islands this cult he joined is on."

"Why can't you say his name? It's Cleve...and whether you like it or not, he's my brother."

"Half-brother," he insisted tightly.

"He's my brother." Her voice was quietly insistent. "I can understand why you won't talk about Mother...she hurt you, but—"

He gave a short grunt. "Not likely. I wouldn't have given a damn if she had taken off with the Ninth Fleet instead of that hot-shot senator. It just means she had lousy taste. But I've heard enough about the kid to know he's bad news. He's been screwed up since day one. I don't like to see you so involved with him."

Rachel walked to the window to stare out over her father's estate with unseeing eyes. How could she make Asa understand that not only did she love Cleve, she had a responsibility to him? At nineteen he was so very young, and so very confused. Since he had been six years old she had spent every one of his birthdays with him, once even running away from boarding school to do it. Since his parents had been away constantly, building the senator's public image, Rachel had always been the one stable thing in Cleve's life. Even if she wanted to, she wouldn't take that away from him.

Turning back to her father, she said, "I'm going, Asa. Nothing you do or say will stop me."

His strong lips tightened. "You said he told that guru idiot he didn't have a family. Won't it be a little bit awkward when you show up? Always supposing you find him in the first place."

"I'll find him," she said. Her chin bore a faint resemblance to his as it firmed in determination. "That's one of the things you taught me, Asa. Money is for getting the impossible done. I'm going to the Marquesas."

Chapter Two

July

It's beautiful, isn't it?''

Rachel glanced at the man who stood beside her at the boat rail and smiled, then turned back to the view. She didn't want to take her eyes from the panorama unfolding before her.

On the far right the island of Tahuata rose from the glistening expanse of water like an irritable giant. And to Rachel's left, on the other side of the narrow Bordelais Channel, was the sight that held her fascinated gaze—the island of Hiva Oa.

Millions of years of erosion had formed razorback ridges and thrusting spires. It looked as though it had been thrown violently into the ocean, its harsh contours smashed into place by an angry fist. The only softening touch was the cover of lush tropical foliage.

Beautiful? she thought. Perhaps. But somehow beauty seemed too pedestrian a word to do it justice. It wasn't anything like the drugging, sensual splendor of Tahiti. Hiva Oa was a breathtaking exaggeration of beauty. A beauty that set every nerve on edge.

"Don't you think we're traveling awfully close to the coastline?"

The hesitant question pulled her gaze back to Mr. White, the man standing beside her. The vacationing Englishman looked slightly green. He and Rachel, along with three other passengers, had left Nuku Hiva early that morning on the ancient boat. Traveling on the open ocean hadn't been exactly smooth, but the water in the channel was even more turbulent, causing the boat to pitch violently.

From directly behind them, one of the crew spoke in French. "The captain does it this way to limit the distance we would need to swim in case of shipwreck."

"What did he say?" Mr. White asked.

When Rachel translated the Englishman blanched. Rachel had caught the twinkle in the Marquesan's eyes and laughed ruefully when the Englishman joined another passenger who was hanging over the rail.

"Don't worry," the crewman said to Rachel. "The ocean will smooth out when we round Teaehoa Point." He pointed to a brutal outcropping of land. "I've come this way every day for thirty years. And the captain has not lost too many tourists yet."

He was right. As soon as they rounded the point the water smoothed out to become shimmering blue bay. They passed coconut palms and pandanus, and the strong, sweet smell of drying copra was overwhelming.

On the quay Mr. White led the passengers in a quick departure. He stood for several minutes trying to find an islander to carry his luggage.

Hiding a smile, Rachel picked up her two small suitcases and began to walk. She had learned on Nuku Hiva that the Marquesans hadn't become obsessed with money as so many South Sea islanders had. Although they were very friendly, they were also independent.

After obtaining directions from a passing woman, Rachel walked the short distance to the bungalow she had rented after calling from Nuku Hiva.

"But only for three days, you understand," the owner said as he handed her the key to the bungalow. "Monsieur and Madame Kamahioli arrive on Friday. They come every year for the Bastille Day celebration."

"Yes, of course. I'm sure I won't need it even that long," she said confidently.

The small bungalow was simple, but charming and extremely clean. Rachel unpacked quickly and stepped into the shower. She felt restless. She should have been able to make arrangements for passage to the Alexandras on Nuku Hiva, but everywhere she turned she had run into problems.

She dried herself off, then began to brush her long hair vigorously. Gradually the strokes slowed as she thought of Cleve and the last time she had seen him. He had been devastated for weeks after the funeral. Then one day he had turned up without notice at her apartment.

For a while he had talked of inconsequentials, but something was different. It was as though a new hope, perhaps a last hope, had been offered to him.

"All right, that's enough small talk," she had said, curling up in the chair opposite him.

She examined his features slowly. At a glance Cleve looked to be about sixteen. There was a softness, a fragility, about Cleve that always worried her. Since the funeral he had seemed even more breakable.

Although physically they resembled each other—both having inherited their mother's blond hair and delicate bone structure—Asa's dominant genes had given Rachel a strength that Cleve was missing.

"Tell me what you're up to," she said coaxingly.

"Up to?" A mischievous gleam shone in his blue eyes. It was a look she hadn't seen since he was a boy. When she shook her fist at him, he laughed. "Okay, okay." He leaned forward eagerly. "I know you've been worried about what I would do now. No, don't deny it. I've seen the way you look at me—like you want to take my temperature. Well, you don't have to worry anymore. Rachel, I want to tell you about it, but you've got to promise to keep an open mind."

She raised one haughty brow. "Since when have I not kept an open mind?"

"I know, but this is different. It may sound a little weird at first, but if you'll just hear me out—"

"Why don't you just tell me about it?"

He drew in a deep breath. "I've joined a cult."

Rachel blinked, trying to keep her feelings from showing, but apparently she didn't succeed.

"I know how that sounds," he said, smiling wryly. "But I promise, I'm not following a man who thinks he's Jesus, or a Hindu visionary. In fact, we haven't discussed religion. Bruce isn't offering a panacea, Rachel. He's merely proposing an alternate life-style."

"Bruce?"

"He's the man who started the whole thing," Cleve said enthusiastically. "I wish you could meet him. He's brilliant and...and so much more. When you look in his eyes it's like you can see forever. And not a forever with nuclear war or ecological disaster hanging over your head. He's offering me a chance to build a new world, one that's based on love and respect rather than power."

"Just exactly where is this new world?" she asked, smiling politely, as though they were holding a perfectly normal conversation.

"That's the great part. It's in the South Pacific, near the Marquesas Islands. No newspapers, no television. Bruce says when the 'civilized' world eventually decides to blow itself to bits we'll be ready to pick up the pieces and start over the right way."

"Bruce's way," she murmured.

"Don't say it like that. I can't tell you the way he told me. If you could just meet him, you'd know that this is something really worthwhile."

"So I'll meet him," she said.

He looked down at his hands, avoiding her eyes.

She laughed, hiding her anxiety. "Come on, Cleve. What are you not telling me?"

Glancing up, he gave her a wry smile. "I told him I had no family," he said bluntly. When he saw the hurt in her eyes he said quickly, "It's not like that, Rachel. I know you're my family. I don't know what I would have done all these years without you. But Bruce won't take anyone who has a family." He leaned toward her in his eagerness to convince her. "He says he can't have people—family or deprogrammers, that sort of thing—invading what he's built. He only wants people who are free to commit themselves totally to the new life."

She was silent for a long time, trying desperately to be objective. She had to be careful not to put him on the defensive. If he began viewing her as the opposition she stood a chance of losing him forever.

Glancing up, she met his eyes. "And you really trust this man?"

"Totally," he said, his voice firm with commitment. "He's not a young freak. He must be at least fifty—but no long hair or wild clothes. His eyes are as gray as his hair. He's tall and strong, but the most important thing is he's really a caring person. You'd like him, Rachel—I know you would. He's sort of a fatherly person."

And that was what was at the core of all Cleve's problems, she thought in regret. Cleve, although he probably didn't know it, was trying to find the love his own father had denied him his whole life. Even when the ambitious senator had managed to spend time at home with him, there had been a coldness in his attitude toward his son—toward all children—that not even a mother's and sister's love could make up for.

In the end she had found there was nothing she could do other than accept Cleve's decision, because technically he was an adult. He had left New York in early March. Two days later she had received a letter postmarked in Los Angeles. In it he told her he was very happy and that his destination was somewhere in the Alexandra Islands. That was when Rachel had begun to make plans for his birthday.

It had all seemed straightforward back then. She would simply fly out for a couple of weeks and see that he was truly happy in his new home. How could she have known she would run into a brick wall at every turn?

The Alexandra Islands were under French control, just as the Marquesas were. She had assumed someone on the large island of Nuku Hiva would know where the cult was located. But no one wanted to speak of the Alexandras. It was almost as though the islands to the south were taboo.

In desperation she tried to hire a plane and pilot to search the islands for her. But again she ran into a dead end. The island plane had a regular schedule, which didn't include the Alexandra Islands, and the pilot wasn't willing to deviate from his course.

When she tried to hire a boat she got the same answers over and over. The Alexandras were too far away; it would take too much time. The answers were always given with great courtesy and with many apologies, but Rachel had sensed that there were other reasons for the Marquesans' refusal to take her to the mysterious islands.

Several boat owners had suggested that Rachel try Hiva Oa. The island was closer to the Alexandras, they said, and she might find someone in Atuona to take her.

Apparently word had gotten around that she was looking for transportation to the Alexandras. On her last day on Nuku Hiva a drunken man had approached her in the street.

"You want to go to the devil islands?" he asked, grinning widely. "Go to Atuona. Flynn will take you." Then he had walked away, laughing wildly.

A recommendation from a drunk was not exactly what she had been looking for, so Rachel had put the incident from her mind. It was simply another dead end in a long line of them.

But now she was in Atuona. The Alexandra Islands were within her reach. She was positive someone here would take her to her brother.

"And I won't rest until I find that someone," she said aloud as she secured her long hair in a twist at the back of her head.

Later, as she wandered about the small capital city, Rachel had difficulty keeping her mind on her brother. Everywhere she looked she saw something new and exciting. The people, with their symmetric, elegant features, were as colorful and dramatic as the scenery.

"*Mademoiselle?* You are looking for guide?" A small boy of eleven or twelve appeared out of nowhere. His French, while not exactly fluent, was understandable. "That's me," he continued, pointing to his thin bare chest. "Tea is the best guide in Atuona."

She smiled down at him. Although he had strong Polynesian features there was a knowing look about him that was the same in New Jersey or Los Angeles. A streetwise kid.

"Actually, I do need some help," she said, taking a coin from her purse.

"Then you are very fortunate that I found you," he said proudly. "I take you to see the graves of Paul Gauguin, the great painter, and Jacques Brel—you've heard of him? All the tourists want to see these. You will have the advantage of being led by an excellent guide."

She chuckled. "I like your style, Tea, but the graves will have to wait. Tell me, is it possible to hire a boat to take me to one of the other islands?"

"Oh sure," he said expansively. "I have many friends who will take you anywhere you want to go. Are you kidding? A beautiful *mademoiselle* like you. They take you with much ecstasy."

Rachel threw back her head and laughed in frank enjoyment. "Tea, I don't know if you're the best guide in Atuona, but I would bet you're the most popular."

He stared for a moment at her laughing face, then said a Polynesian word she didn't understand. "Sheesh, you're some hot stuff," he added in French.

"I think we'd better talk about the boat," she said dryly. "Which of your many friends do you recommend to take me to the Alexandras?"

"No, no." He shook his head emphatically. "You don't want to go there. I get my cousin to take you to Fatu Híva. You will like it there. Many tourists go there. Or perhaps you would like to go around Hiva Oa to Paumau. They say the old ones still walk there." He smiled, his perfect white teeth glinting in the sunlight. "Me, I've never seen them, but maybe you'll have more luck."

"I haven't got time to see Fatu Hiva or Paumau right now," she explained. "I need someone to take me to the Alexandras."

Tea wasn't smiling now. His dark eyes were worried as he stared up at her. "But no one goes there. It is impossible."

She gave him a skeptical glance. "Someone must go there sometime. They can't be completely cut off from the world. Surely there's a supply boat or something."

He shrugged. "Those are things I don't know. I only know no one from Hiva Oa goes there. You won't hire anyone here. Unless..." His voice trailed away indecisively.

"Yes?" she said eagerly. "You've thought of someone who will take me?"

He shrugged doubtfully. "I don't know. Maybe Flynn."

Flynn again. Tea's recommendation wasn't much better than the drunken man's on Nuku Hiva. She sighed. Needs must, she thought, because the devil was definitely driving.

"This man Flynn," she said in resignation, "do you think he'll take me to the Alexandras?"

"Flynn, he's—" Tea broke off and tapped his forehead, making his meaning clear. "He might take you on the *Nightingale*. Maybe. If he drinks enough *okolehao* today. Who can tell with Flynn?"

She inhaled slowly. At least it was a place to start. "How can I find Mr. Flynn?"

"I take you. But me, I think you are making one big mistake. Fatu Hiva is much nicer." He grinned up at her. "But I am only here to serve you. I will guide you to Pigalle." Motioning, he began to walk away.

"Pigalle?" she queried, hurrying to keep up.

"That is not its real name, of course," Tea said over his shoulder. "But it had been called so for many years—for as long as I can remember."

"Many years, huh?" she asked, laughing.

He nodded seriously. "My mother says Parisian sailors have give it this name. When the sailors left, the name remained."

"And Mr. Flynn lives in Pigalle?"

"He is not Mr. Flynn. He is just Flynn. Sometimes he lives on his sailing boat, which is of a beauty *formidable*."

"The *Nightingale*?" she asked, remembering the name he had used earlier.

"*Oui*, he calls it that." He glanced up at her. "This is a bird, *non*?" When she nodded, he continued. "He also keeps a room over Fauzy's bar. This is not a place of elegance. Your bungalow is much nicer. Fauzy gets the men drunk, then rents them a room when they pass out." He made a clucking sound. "That Fauzy, he's one sharp businessman."

"I'm all admiration," she said dryly.

"Come," he said, picking up her hand to pull her along. "It's this way."

Five minutes later they turned a corner and entered another world. Pigalle had a flavor that was different from the rest of Atuona. Buildings with corrugated tin roofs were closely spaced on both sides of the street, the shabby exteriors garishly painted.

Rachel's young guide pulled her past several short alleys that were being steadily reclaimed by the jungle. In some of them naked and near-naked children played. Their squeals of laughter needed no translation. The sound was the same all over the world. In one short alley an emaciated old man slept comfortably in the shadows. A silver mist of whiskers covered his deeply lined face. The small insects that flew in and out of the cavern of his mouth didn't disturb his dreams.

"Ginger's Place," Tea said, bringing her attention to a bright turquoise building.

A lovely young Japanese girl sat on the porch in a sagging chair made of some woven material. One foot was propped on the porch railing, her knee bent. The robe was loosely cinched, exposing most of her small, firm breasts. Her face showed intense concentration as she leaned forward to paint her toenails pink.

In the middle of the street, before a wooden easel, a thin black man sat on a stool and also painted the girl's toenails. For a moment Rachel stood behind the artist and stared at the portrait of one small, Oriental foot; then she let Tea pull her away.

"Will I tell you what kind of establishment is Ginger's?" he asked, grinning broadly.

She cocked an eyebrow. "How old are you, Tea?"

"Next week I will have ten years. That's almost a man, *n'est-ce pas*?"

"In your case, I would agree."

He nodded seriously, then stopped walking. "This is it," Tea said.

He indicated a pink building at the end of the street. Except for the painted glass in the windows it was a duplicate of the other buildings, but it sat away from them slightly. The lush tropical jungle crept up behind and around it. On the front of the two-story structure was a sign painted in childish stick letters: Le Hotel et Lounge de Fauzy.

Rachel stared at it for a moment, then dug into her purse for money. "You've been very helpful, Tea."

She smiled. "I promise to recommend you to everyone I meet."

"For you, beautiful *mademoiselle*, it has been more pleasure than business," he said, then took the money she offered and ran off down the street.

Rachel shook her head, watching until he was out of sight. It wouldn't surprise her to learn that the enterprising Tea had a Swiss bank account and a sizable stock portfolio.

The front door of Fauzy's opened directly onto the bar. Rachel stepped inside and for a moment she thought it was cooler; then she realized it was only the darkness that gave the illusion of a drop in temperature.

A ceiling fan moved sluggishly, turning just fast enough to disturb the flies that were buzzing around the only two customers in the room. Behind a long wooden counter a large, dark man wiped at a glass, his movements as sluggish as the fan's. With wrinkled khaki slacks he wore a white ribbed sleeveless undershirt, dark stains showing under each arm. Rising from the neck of the low-cut undershirt was the top of a large, elaborate tattoo.

He didn't even look up as Rachel entered, but kept on drying the glasses on a wooden tray as he listened to a scratchy recording that might once have been Ella Fitzgerald.

Only when she stood directly in front of him did the man finally glance up, acknowledging her presence. He ran his gaze over her with lazy disinterest before he said, "A drink, *mademoiselle*?"

She shook her head. "I'm looking for a man named Flynn. Do you know him?"

For an instant his dark eyes showed anger, then banked to suspicion. "Why do you look for Flynn?"

Puzzled, she said, "I need to talk to him . . . about business."

Making a sound that could have meant anything, he dropped his gaze to a fly that had just landed on the counter. "Business?" As he spoke, he wound the stained towel into a taut rope. He swatted the fly with a sharp smack, then glanced at Rachel. "If he owes you money I would advise you to forget it, *mademoiselle*."

Rachel inhaled, forcing herself to remain calm in the face of his patently rude behavior. "He doesn't owe me money."

The bartender snorted loudly. "You are perhaps the only person on Hiva Oa who can say that."

Rachel slowly placed her arms on the bar. Anyone who knew her even slightly would have been wary of the tilt of her chin. Slowly, carefully, she said, "Monsieur Fauzy, does Mr. Flynn keep a room at your establishment?"

"Yes . . ." The word was slow and languid. Monsieur Fauzy was unfortunately not someone who knew her even slightly. "But not for much longer. I give him one more day. Then, if his bill is not paid, he is gone."

It was a step forward, she thought. A small one to be sure, but enough to keep her from exploding. "And is he by any chance here now?"

Fauzy shook his head contemptuously. "He has not the courage to face me. He will probably sneak in when my back is turned." He scratched his chest. "You could try Ginger's, but I don't suppose he's paid his bill there, either."

Ginger's. That was the turquoise house with the beautiful Japanese girl. Although Rachel wouldn't balk at tackling a Polynesian cathouse, she decided she would exhaust the other possibilities first.

"*Monsieur*, would it be possible for me to wait for Mr. Flynn here?"

He shrugged in unconcern. "If you buy a drink; I don't care if you stay until I retire."

When she ordered mineral water he shook his head morosely and, to punish her for ordering such a cheap drink, put one stingy piece of ice in the liquid. Rachel carried the glass to a table toward the back of the bar, where she had a clear view of the door.

The two men who had been in the bar when she arrived had watched silently during her conversation with Fauzy. Now they followed her movements with their eyes, speaking to each other in low whispers. One of them burst out laughing, and they turned in their chairs to stare at her, grinning openly.

When one of them shouted "*Ma'm'selle,*" and began making crude kissing noises, Rachel glanced at the surly bartender, but she could have been invisible as far as he was concerned.

After enduring their boorish behavior for almost five minutes she had had enough. Standing abruptly, she again approached the bar.

"Monsieur Fauzy," she said firmly. "I don't believe I'll wait here after all. I would like to wait in Mr. Flynn's room."

He slowly raised one heavy eyebrow. "You think I let any stranger into my customers' rooms? What if you wish to steal something? Flynn is a guest here...even if he is a miserable *bâtard* who doesn't pay his bill."

"I don't want to steal anything. I told you I wanted to talk to him about business. I wish to hire him." She paused, studying his face. "He could make enough money from me to pay your bill," she said slyly.

The argument swayed him. "Very well," he said finally. "You can wait in his room, but remember, *mademoiselle*, I can identify you. If you steal, there is no place to hide on Hiva Oa."

She bit her tongue to keep back a stinging retort. Cleve, she thought as she followed the man upstairs, you're going to pay for this, little brother.

Upstairs the bartender opened a door with a key from a large ring tied to his belt with a shoestring. Rachel moved past him into the room, not even bothering to glance up when Fauzy closed the door and left.

The room was a disaster. The clothes and newspapers scattered carelessly about couldn't hide the thick layer of dust. Dull-looking sheets hung off the edge of the bed.

This room belonged to the man she wanted to hire? she thought as she inhaled the musty odor.

Gingerly removing clothes from the only chair in the room, she sat down. She wasn't hiring him to be neat, she decided, trying not to think about what might be living under the clutter. She merely wanted him to take her to Cleve.

Smiling slightly, Rachel let her head rest against the wall. Cleve would be so surprised to see her. She could just picture him, all brown and strong from work and sun. She shouldn't have worried so much about him. This hiatus from the pressures of life was probably just exactly what he needed. Soon Cleve would realize that he was strong enough to reenter the real world.

She fell asleep thinking of a future where she and her brother were business partners, building hotels and condos on lush tropical islands.

Chapter Three

Flynn leaned against the wall of Hang So's laundry for support as he stared at Fauzy's bar. He could hear raucous laughter inside, and for a moment he thought it was a shame he couldn't join them. But only for a moment. He didn't often push his limits with alcohol—well, not too often anyway—but tonight he knew he had had enough.

When three men approached the bar Flynn stepped in behind them. As they entered the smoke-filled room he kept his head down low. Casting his gaze quickly around the bar, he spotted Fauzy in the corner of the room, carrying on a vigorous argument.

Good old Fauzy, he thought as he ducked out of sight in the stairway. One of these days Flynn would have to pay his gracious landlord.

Halfway up the stairs he tripped and muttered "Shh" as he held a warning finger to his lips. At the door to his room he tried for several minutes to insert the key. When he grasped the knob to keep it from moving out of range, it turned in his hand and the door swung open.

"Thank you very much," he said, nodding politely to the door.

Inside the room he stopped as abruptly as he could manage in his condition. "Wait a minute," he said, leaning forward to peer into the dark room. "I think there's someone in my room . . . said the Papa bear."

You're in your room, stupid.

He shook his head argumentatively. "No, I mean someone besides me." Someone—a woman—stood up from the chair beside his bed. Flynn swayed slightly, then tried to pull himself up straight. He put a hand to his head, hoping the action would keep the room from spinning around him.

"Okay," he said, waving at the blurred figure before him. "The one in the middle can stay. The rest of you come back some other time."

He chuckled softly at his own joke and stepped closer. "Who're you?" Squinting, he leaned his head slightly forward. Then he held up one hand and shook his head. "No—no, don't tell me. Flynn's keen wits do not crumble even in the midst of an alcoholic stupor. Yes, I've got it," he said, nodding in satisfaction. "Fancy Nancy is expecting her sister—" He broke off abruptly. "People who aren't feeling well shouldn't be forced to say S's," he muttered. "You're Nancy's sister from Australia, right?"

He inhaled expansively, pleased at having solved the puzzle. Then, stepping even closer, he frowned. "You don't look much like Nancy. Her hair is black...all over it's black. I could check to see if your hair is black in other places."

Flynn felt a wave of dizziness sweep over. Damn Pete. Flynn knew better than to try to keep up with him. Everyone knew Pete had a cast-iron stomach.

"What? Did you say something?" he said vaguely.

Flynn was almost sure she was speaking, but the sound was merely a buzzing in his head. He wanted his bed; he wanted it very much. As he took a step toward it, he remembered the woman in his room.

"Look, honey, I'm real sorry. I'd sure like to make you welcome, but the truth is I'm flat broke." He patted his pockets distractedly as he moved toward the bed. "I don't even have anything to sell except my watch. I told Ginger...I told her I couldn't afford any yum-yum for a while."

At that moment the moon came out from behind a cloud. A shaft of silver light poured in through the window, illuminating the woman who stood not two feet away from him. Her golden hair, shot with pure silver, almost blinded him. Sucking in a startled breath, Flynn stopped moving and stared.

Standing before him was the most beautiful woman he had ever seen. No, he thought dazedly, that wasn't true. Her features weren't perfect. Her mouth was just a shade too wide, her chin just a hair too strong. Her breasts, although firm and round, were too small, her legs too long and coltish. But somehow all the features came together in a picture that dazzled him.

As he stared in bemusement Flynn felt that old familiar feeling tugging at his loins. Reaching out unsteadily, he stroked the clean line of her cheek with one finger.

"On second thought," he murmured, his voice deep and husky with desire, "I don't have any appointments to keep. Why do I need a watch?"

Jerking her into his arms, he fell backward, pulling the woman with him across the bed.

Rachel made a strangled sound in the back of her throat. What in hell did he think he was doing? she thought, livid with indignation. She fought the body pressing into hers. She fought the hands that seemed to cling to her like seaweed. He grunted when she slammed her fist into his kidneys, but didn't loosen his hold.

No man got the better of Rachel McNaught, she thought in fury. No man.

She was breathing hard when, moments later, he held her hands above her head and straddled her waist.

"Let me explain things." His voice was slurred and breathless. "You see, you can't be this energetic when a man's had too much to drink. It's wearing me out." When she turned her head and bit his arm, he sucked in a sharp breath. "Ginger messed up good this time," he muttered to himself. "It's old Tom who likes his lovin' rough."

Holding both her hands in one large fist, he reached down to cup her breast. "But there's no mistake here," he whispered huskily. "I've just decided this is exactly the way I like it." He paused for a second, then grinned. "Maybe it would be all right to play rough just once."

"You mangy bast—"

Rachel's words were cut off when he lowered his mouth to hers. She felt his tongue invade her mouth; it tasted of whiskey. It tasted of man. Then, moving with an agility that surprised her, he slid down until he lay full length against her, still holding her hands above her head.

When she felt him growing hard against her, rage exploded inside her head. She stopped struggling and sank her teeth fiercely into his lower lip.

"Son of a bitch!" he gasped, seeking the wound with his tongue. "You little hellcat. I said you could play rough, but I didn't say anything about mutilating me."

When he let go of her hands to touch the cut on his lip with his forefinger, Rachel shoved with all her strength. Flailing wildly, he fell off the bed and landed on the floor with a hard thud.

She scrambled from the mattress, panting harshly. Her hair had come undone in the struggle and fell wildly around her flushed face. Brushing it back with a rough stroke, she stared at the man sitting on the floor.

She had never in her life lost control of her emotions; it was something she took great pride in. But now, with this man, Rachel lost control. She drew back her foot and, with all her strength, kicked him.

"Hellfire! Stop that!" he yelped, sliding backward away from her kick.

Rachel's lips twisted in a slightly feral smile. He was cornered and couldn't move out of her range. She felt a surge of pure pagan pleasure when her toe connected with his thigh, then his hip.

"Judas Priest! Will you quit? All right...all right," he said, raising a hand as he watched her warily. "I take it all back. You're not a hellcat." He slid closer to the wall and rubbed his thigh. "But if it's all the same to you, I think I'll leave you to old Tom."

"Mr. Flynn," she said between her teeth. The words sounded rough to her own ears. "Will you listen to me carefully? Maybe, just maybe, your alcohol-corroded brain can take this in." She gulped in air to steady her breathing, then said slowly, emphatically, "I do not now, and have not ever, known the person you call Ginger. I am not Fancy Nancy's sister, and may I say I highly resent the implication. And, please understand this, I am *not* yum-yum."

Flynn stared at her for a moment in silence. "Well, well, well," he said softly, picking himself up off the floor. He seemed to be sobering up fast. "Definitely not Australian." His gaze ran over her from top to bottom. "If I'm not mistaken it's a genuine Back Bay, back-biting, Boston rich bitch. Bryn Mawr accent and all." He stepped closer. "I should have recognized the nose." When he reached out to touch her nose Rachel jerked away furiously. "Always positioned to look down on someone," he added lightly.

"Kindly keep your hands to yourself," she said tightly, raising her chin. "And I should have recognized an unkempt, uncouth *pig*. We have them even in Boston. People who can't make it in the real world, so they drop out and live by sponging off others."

She pushed her unruly hair back again with an unsteady hand, already regretting her loss of control. "Forget I said that," she said briskly. "Maybe we should start over. I came here to charter your boat." She ran her gaze over him, as he had done to her moments before. "From what I hear, you can't afford to offend a prospective customer, Mr. Flynn."

He stood perfectly still for a moment. Then he moved to flick on the light switch. Rachel almost flinched when she saw the anger in his dark eyes.

It was her first chance to really examine the man who had handled her so intimately. He was unshaven, uncombed and probably unbathed. But a curious twinge attacked the pit of her stomach as she stared at him. The strength she saw in his arms and chest and thighs was already familiar to her. She had felt it moments before. It was a strange sensation, this familiarity. She had felt his strength, but why did she think she knew his features as well.

She had never met this man Flynn, whose dark hair curled untidily on the back of his neck, whose face was square and harshly chiseled. When she saw the purplish swelling on his lip she glanced away from it quickly and met his blazing blue eyes.

Then in an instant his anger disappeared in a smile. Before she could stop him, he reached out to grab her roughly, pulling her body close to his. His lips were hard and punishing on hers. To her shame, it was a moment before she began to struggle for her freedom.

"And I think," he said softly, his breath warm against her lips, "that you need lessons in how to be human."

"Why you—"

"But not from me," he continued, letting her go so abruptly that she fell back against the door.

He walked to the bed and sprawled full-length on top of it, his hands linked casually behind his head. "I haven't got the inclination or the time to spend on a Boston-baked belle." He grinned and, mimicking her accent, added, "I'll have to pass on this prospective customer."

Rachel felt rage whip through her. Whirling, she jerked open the door. She was almost through it when she stopped reluctantly.

What was she doing? She couldn't let this chance go just because the man had the manners of a bush ape. And, to be perfectly fair, she had been in his room in the darkness when he arrived. If she hadn't been so groggy with sleep, and if he hadn't been so intoxicated, she could have explained her presence. Then the unpleasant episode would never have occurred. She didn't want to think of what had happened on his bed, but logically she knew that, given his strength, he could have done much more.

She turned around slowly to face him. "That was very well done, Mr. Flynn. You called my bluff. I need you more than you need me." She met his gaze squarely. "I need transportation to the Alexandras badly. My brother is on one of the islands." She shrugged wearily. "I don't know which one, but I would like to hire you to help me find him."

It was as though she hadn't spoken. He merely stared at her in silence.

She closed the door and leaned against it. "We got off to a bad start. I realize it was partly my fault." She drew in a steadying breath. She hated apologizing to this man, but she would do whatever was necessary to get to Cleve for his birthday. "You don't like me—that's your privilege. But surely, out of feeling for a fellow human being, you could do something to help me."

He smiled lazily. It was the first sign that he even recognized the fact that she was speaking. "I used to be human," he murmured, "but luckily I got over it."

In defeat, she let out the breath she had been holding. "If you can't take me to the Alexandras, could you at least recommend someone who can?"

He didn't speak for a moment as he studied her expression. Rachel knew her anxiety showed on her face, and she very much resented letting him see it.

"I'm afraid you're out of luck." There was nothing gloating about his tone; it was matter of fact. "No one will take you. You'd better go back home."

"But you don't under—"

"Go home, lady," he said abruptly, as though something about her was beginning to irritate him. "I can't help you." When she didn't move he ran his gaze over her body in a blatant insult. "If you're going to stay in my room you'd damn well better get in my bed."

Whirling around, she jerked open the door and walked out, the sound of his laughter pursuing her down the stairs.

Chapter Four

At fifteen minutes until six the next morning Rachel stuffed her billfold into the pocket of her loose cotton slacks and left the bungalow. As she walked through the curiously empty streets her features were fixed in determination.

When she had left Pigalle the night before she had been tired and discouraged. She had even considered calling her father. He could have a plane and pilot on Hiva Oa within a day. But she knew without asking that Asa wouldn't make it that easy for her. There were a thousand delaying tactics he could use to keep her from reaching Cleve by his birthday.

This morning she was astonished that she had even considered Asa a possibility. She would find Cleve if she had to buy a boat and sail it herself. But she wasn't that desperate yet. There had to be someone on Hiva Oa who could take her to the Alexandras. And if such a person existed, she would find him today. She didn't need Asa . . . or Flynn.

At six o'clock exactly doors began to open and a sudden flow of people rushed past her. On foot, on motorcycles and in cars, they all seemed to have one destination. Curious, Rachel followed the crowd. She laughed aloud when she found that their goal was a Chinese bakery.

Mountains of crisp, fragrant French bread were snatched up in armloads by the villagers. With a when-in-Rome shrug Rachel took her place in the bustling throng, deciding that one of the *baguettes* would make a perfect breakfast. After picking up a cup of strong, hot coffee at an open air café, she sat near the town hall for her meal in the sun.

As she looked around her, Rachel decided it was no wonder she hadn't heard from Cleve. If the Alexandras were anything like the Marquesas, he was probably mesmerized by the sheer beauty of his surroundings.

As she finished her coffee, she watched a group of children hoist a makeshift flag. The flowers and children and sky combined in a riotous display of color.

"Allons enfants de la Patrie, Le jour de gloire est arrive," they sang in their mock celebration of Bastille Day.

After feeding the remainder of the bread to the birds, she stood and brushed the crumbs from her hands. Gazing around, she frowned. Where did she start? The docks seemed the most logical place, but so many of the Marquesans spoke only their native Polynesian language. Unless she found an interpreter she would be lost.

At that moment she spotted a young boy coming around the corner of a building. Under his arm he held a small, battered fighting cock. Rachel smiled slowly. Now she knew where she would begin.

Raising a hand, she shouted "Tea!" as she hurried to catch up with him.

Rachel carried both her suitcases as she walked along Pigalle toward Fauzy's bar. Her chin was not quite so firm today. She had thought surely by the time the regular guests showed up to claim her bungalow she would have found someone to help her. But in the past forty-eight hours she felt she had spoken—singly and in groups—to every person on the island of Hiva Oa. And everywhere she'd turned she'd met resistance.

The first day of her search, Tea had eagerly introduced Rachel to his cousin Tana, a bright young athlete who stood almost six feet tall. According to Tana, it would be his pleasure to take her to the other side of the island, to Paumau, where a "crazy Englishman" in the company of his wife and friends had moored his yacht. Tea and Tana seemed to think a foreigner might just be crazy enough to take Rachel to the Alexandras.

The trip across the island was an acrophobic's nightmare. Tana, smiling sweetly the whole time, drove like all the demons of hell were in pursuit. As the jeep climbed rapidly Tea identified mango, pandanus and ironwood trees for her, shouting at the top of his lungs to be heard over the roar of the engine and the wind.

After a while, feeling dizzy with the speed and the boy's travelogue, Rachel kept her eyes trained on the green buttresses that radiated from the island's razor-sharp crest down to the sea in every direction.

As they slid around a curve she caught a glimpse of the coast. The sun filled the bays with splashes of silver and azure. She gasped in pleasure, then immediately squeezed her eyes shut when, at top speed, they crossed a natural bridge, steep slopes falling away on each side.

It was only for the descent that Tana slowed. The hairpin curves were so sharp that he had to maneuver the jeep back and forth above a precipice at each bend. After the first time she decided this was an event that also called for closed eyes.

Given the hair-raising quality of the drive, Rachel felt an extra touch of exhilaration as they dropped past valleys filled with coconut trees and tiny villages of no more than two or three houses.

Then, without warning, she got her first look at the spectacular bay rimmed with white-sand beach. She touched Tea's arm and pointed to a large white yacht anchored in the bay. He stood up in the back seat of the jeep, holding a hand over his eyes to block out the glare of the sun.

Smiling broadly, he nodded. "That's it!" he shouted over the wind.

Rachel stared at the large, elegant rig. Would it be her ticket to the Alexandras?

Now, in Pigalle, she smiled grimly at the memory. Setting down the heavy suitcases, she flexed her fingers, then picked up her luggage again and continued walking.

She had spent the best part of the first day being sickeningly sweet to the most obnoxious people she had ever set eyes on, only to be told late in the day that they were leaving in a few hours for Tahiti.

I will not be defeated, she thought stubbornly. She had gone to all this trouble to spend Cleve's birthday with him, and, come hell or high water, she would do just exactly that.

Breathing in deeply, she climbed the steps to Fauzy's bar, shifted the suitcases to one arm and opened the door.

Flynn saw the woman as soon as she walked into the bar. Leaning back in his chair, he studied her over the top of his beer. She wasn't exactly hard to spot. Her casual cotton slacks and blouse had designer written all over them. Even if she had been dressed in a flour sack, the delicate lines of her face and the sleekness of her hair would have shouted breeding and elegance. She looked as out of place in the dissolute splendor of Fauzy's bar as Flynn would at a debutante's ball.

Rachel McNaught, he thought as he watched her. She was causing a lot of talk in Atuona. He had heard this morning that she was still on the island and had thought at the time that she was incredibly stupid. That she was also incredibly beautiful hadn't escaped him, but it didn't change the facts.

Her chin, tilted ever so slightly, held the same haughty determination he had run into during his own encounter with her. He hadn't noticed then that her eyes were green. He noticed now. He also noticed the look in them. She hadn't given up.

But sooner or later she would, he told himself. She wouldn't find anyone on Hiva Oa to take her to the Alexandras. In fact, she wouldn't find anyone on any of the islands. And all her money couldn't buy what the Marquesans didn't want to sell—in this case, their time and service.

He frowned, thinking of the talk he had heard around town. There were more rumors than usual concerning the mysterious island group to the south. Vague rumors about trouble.

Although officially the Marquesans governed the Alexandras, unofficially neither group recognized the other. Somewhere in the ancient past there had been wars and blood feuds between the two. And in the Marquesas, the past was very much a part of the present.

For a moment, as he stared at Rachel, he considered filling her in on the facts; then he shrugged and turned his attention to some men at the next table. Boston socialites weren't in his line of work. He knew trouble when he saw it and had always made it a firm policy to stay as far away from it as possible.

Rachel stood for a moment just inside the door. As soon as her eyes adjusted to the darkened room she saw Flynn. He sat at a table across the room, his head thrown back as he laughed at something the large bartender had told him. Cynically Rachel wondered if he had sold his watch to pay Fauzy's bill.

Straightening her shoulders, she walked across the room, stopping beside Fauzy. The laughter died immediately, and both men turned to look at her.

"*Monsieur*," she said quietly, "I seem to be in need of lodging. Have you an available room?"

For a moment the bartender didn't speak; he simply stared at her with a curious expression on his face. Then he shrugged. "Why not? I take money from whoever wishes to give it to me." He turned away. "Come, I will show you."

When she moved to follow him, Rachel felt a hand on her arm, the fingers gripping just tightly enough to prevent her leaving. She glanced at Flynn, then down to the large tanned hand on her upper arm.

"You're making a mistake," he said bluntly. "This is no place for you. Go home."

Her chin rose in an unconscious reaction to his tone. "Will you take me to the Alexandras?"

"No way."

She jerked her arm away. "Then we don't have anything to talk about."

Turning away, she hurried to catch up with her new landlord, who had disappeared with her suitcases.

The room upstairs was a depressing duplicate of Flynn's, but Rachel knew she had no other choice. Streaks of late afternoon sunlight came through the shutters, highlighting dust and heaven only knew what else that floated about in the air.

One thing was certain, she decided. She would spend as little time here as possible. Grabbing her purse, she left the room. In the bar, more customers had arrived. Flynn stood laughing and talking in the center of a group of men. When his eyes met hers across the room she glanced away, quickening her steps as she left the building.

Although her appetite had deserted her, she ordered an elaborate dinner at a restaurant near the bay, lingering over each course to kill time. As she sipped at a glass of wine the sun set in an ever changing display of warm, vibrant colors. Almost immediately it was fully dark.

By the time Rachel returned to Pigalle the community was in full swing. For many this was the beginning of the workday. Leaning against a porch in a tight red dress was the Japanese woman Rachel had seen her first day on the island. The young woman was surrounded by three French sailors, and her laughter floated through the night.

When Rachel walked into the bar noise hit her in a solid wall. The room was filled with smoke and people and an occasional flying bottle.

So much for sleep, she thought wryly as she walked up the stairs to her room.

As she undressed the music and laughter seemed to seep in through cracks in the floor, filling her room. Even with the pillow over her head she heard it. But she must have been more tired than she had realized. Not long after crawling into the lumpy bed she fell into a sound sleep.

When Rachel awoke in the middle of the night the first thing she became aware of was the large hand covering her mouth. A few heart-thumping seconds passed before she realized that a body also covered hers . . . a heavy, male body.

Her eyes jerked open in fear as she screamed beneath the pressing fingers. But only a faint sound emerged. Gasping for air, she heard people shouting. At first she thought the party downstairs was still in full swing; then she realized the angry shouts were coming from the hall directly outside her room.

She struggled frantically to move, trying to throw off the constricting heaviness, but she was pinned securely.

"It's me," a voice whispered. "Don't scream."

When the pressure of his hand eased she jerked her head to the side, gulping in air. "Flynn? *You cretin!* What in hell do you think you're doing? Why—"

She broke off when the voices in the hall got louder, more violent. Through the darkness she could barely distinguish a flash of white teeth as he grinned.

"My creditors," he said in a low voice. "Somehow I get the idea they're beginning to doubt my ability to pay."

"Why are you in my room?" she asked through clenched teeth. "And how did you get in, anyway? Does that stupid bartender hand out keys just for the asking?

"Didn't he tell you that all the keys fit all the doors?"

"No, he definitely didn't tell me. If he had I never would have..."

The words died away in her throat. He was still pressed closely against her, close enough for her to feel the physical changes in his lower body. A sound of rage came from deep in her throat.

"Get off me, you ass!"

"Shh," he said. "They'll hear you."

"Do you think I give a damn what they hear? I will not have you taking pleasure from this."

"I can't help it," he said. The innocence in his voice made her blood boil. "It's an involuntary reaction...like hiccuping, or sneezing."

She closed her eyes tightly and said in a tone of deadly calm, "Just get off me, and then tell me why you're here."

"Do you still want someone to take you to the Alexandras?" he asked without moving.

The quietly spoken question brought her head up with a jerk. She stared at him through the darkness.

"Why do you want to know?" she asked suspiciously.

"It just so happens that my boat has suddenly become available." He paused. "I could take you to the Alexandras for . . . say a thousand dollars."

"That's highway robbery, and you know it!"

"Have you found anyone else to take you?"

She didn't answer. He knew good and well she had found no one on the island to help her.

After a moment he said, "The price is a thousand dollars . . . and I need the full amount tonight so I can stock up on supplies."

"One quarter tonight, and the rest when we get back."

"Half now, and you've got yourself a deal."

Reluctantly she nodded.

He grinned again and rolled away from her to sit on the side of the bed.

She bit her lip. "I don't have that much in cash."

"We cheerfully accept traveler's checks."

"Somehow I guessed you would." Sitting up, she picked up her purse from the floor beside the bed. She tried to find the correct amount, but it was hopeless in the darkness. Moving to the window, she opened the shutters just enough to see what she was doing; then she swung around to face him.

"Before I give you this, tell me when we can leave."

"Meet me at the quay at nine o'clock sharp tomorrow morning and we'll be on our way."

Gritting her teeth, she reluctantly handed him the money. Something didn't feel right. She was getting the same aching twinge in her stomach that she always got when a business deal was going bad.

She heard movement and glanced up. She had expected Flynn to leave by the door, but she hadn't taken his creditors into account. He stepped to the window, grabbed her by the neck and kissed her hard.

"To seal the deal," he said. He stepped back, laughing as she swung wildly. Then, slinging his legs over the sill, he disappeared into the night.

"I hope you break your neck," she whispered vehemently.

She told herself she only imagined the echoing laugh that floated in the air. For a long time she stood staring into the night, a frown worrying her lips. Then suddenly she turned away, a stubborn look gleaming in her green eyes.

Flynn's steps were light and eager as he made his way down the dock to where the *Nightingale* was moored. He spared a momentary thought to whether or not he felt guilty about taking the socialite's money and decided he didn't, not a bit. He would pay her back when he could, and if he couldn't, it wouldn't break her.

As he approached the boat a man's head appeared above the companionway. "You're a little late," the young Polynesian said. "How come you tell me to meet you here at midnight, then don't show up until two?"

"Business, Pete, important business," Flynn said as he jumped the rail to stand beside the other man.

Pete stood a head shorter than Flynn, his straight black hair reaching almost to his shoulders. Tonight he wore a western-cut shirt with the sleeves cut off and khaki shorts. He looked like a Hawaiian beach bum, but he was a genius at mechanics. Pete was Flynn's friend, his comrade at arms, his first mate, and his fellow hellion. They had been through some rough times together, times rough enough to let a man's true character show through. Flynn had seen the essence of Pete more than once and knew it was strong and true.

Taking a bill out of his breast pocket, he handed it to his friend. "I want you to rustle old Claude out of his bed and stock up on supplies. We're off to other ports for a while."

Pete looked at the hundred dollar bill and whistled through his teeth. "You murder a rich American?"

Flynn grinned. "How many times have I told you that violence is not necessary when one has charm?"

"And charm is not necessary when one has brass knuckles," Pete added. "No fooling, where did you get this?"

"Let's just say that one of my many business ventures has finally paid off."

"So why are we absconding in the middle of the night?"

"I'll explain the details later. Right now I want you to get the supplies. I'll take care of the fuel."

"Aye, aye, Captain." Pete jumped agilely over the railing and started to walk away. Glancing back, he said, "I'll go, but I wish you would tell me who I'm supposed to avoid—the gendarmes or a jealous husband?"

Flynn chuckled, then stood for a moment looking around the boat. The neatness, the shine of it, made a sharp contrast to his room over Fauzy's bar. Flynn never allowed the *Nightingale* to fall into disrepair. Even if he had to go without food, his boat got what it needed. It was his home, his only home.

Turning, he stepped over the rail and walked into the night. He had to rouse someone to supply them with extra fuel.

When Flynn returned to the *Nightingale* more than an hour had passed. He had awakened a young Marquesan, who had promised to stand by the fuel pump until they arrived.

Stepping onto the deck, he paused to listen. The gentle lapping of waves against the hull was the only sound he heard, but his neck itched the way it always did when something wasn't right.

"Pete?" he called out softly.

Moving silently, he pulled a knife from his pocket and opened it. As he took the first step down the companionway he said, "Pete, are you here?"

He had taken two steps into the cabin when he stopped abruptly. Rachel was sitting on one of the bunks, her hands folded in her lap as though she were attending a tea party. Two suitcases sat on the bunk beside her.

"It's about time you showed up," she said pleasantly. "Pete and I were tired of waiting." She turned toward the door of the head. "Weren't we, Pete?"

"You bet." The words were muffled, as though Pete was leaning against the door.

"What's he doing in there?"

She picked up a small silver derringer. "He decided he would be more comfortable in there. Didn't you, Pete?"

"Right again," he called out.

She stood up. "Pete and I were talking—just idle chitchat, you understand—and he told me your plans." She smiled. "You know, I think leaving tonight is an excellent idea. That way we avoid the rush-hour traffic."

"The gun's not really necessary," he said, watching her closely.

"Probably not." She shrugged. "But it got me acquainted with Pete a lot quicker. Didn't it, Pete?"

"We're like brother and sister," he said through the door. Now they could hear the laughter in his voice.

Flynn walked to the door of the head and jerked it open. "Come out of there and stop acting like a parrot."

"A lady pulls a gun on me and I'll act like a freakin' dodo bird if it'll keep her happy," Pete said cheerfully.

He moved to sit at the dining alcove opposite Rachel, leaning back casually as he watched the other two people in the boat. "I think we got us a passenger, boss."

Without glancing at Rachel, Flynn said, "You know how often we've said we'd like to explore the Alexandras?"

Pete nodded seriously. "We must say that at least twice a day."

Flynn inhaled. "I guess now is as good a time as any."

Rachel stood on the deck of the boat and gazed around. A full moon flooded the ocean with silvery light, to the west outlining the island of Tahuata, a gigantic black fortress brooding over the waves. To the east was Mohotani. Hiva Oa, two hours behind them, dropped steadily into the ocean.

The *Nightingale* rose and sank gracefully with each swell, and every passing minute took Rachel closer to her goal. To the two men hard at the business of sailing the boat, Rachel knew she appeared calm and collected, but inside her heart raced. Finally, at last, she was on her way.

Chapter Five

These are the Alexandras." Flynn stood beside the spotlighted chart, pointing to a sprinkling of dots. "Four islands. Mana Kula, Pohukaina, Iaukea, and Kamahele. We'll hit Kamahele first—it's the only one I know for certain is inhabited. A missionary who lives there was in Atuona a couple of years ago. He's been on the island for thirty years and is a little batty."

He turned off the light above the charts. "It'll take us a little better than two days to reach Kamahele. In that time you will do what I say, when I say. Got it?"

Rachel stared at him. Pete was topside at the wheel while Captain Bligh went over the details with her in the cabin. She smiled stiffly. "Don't you think that's just a wee bit high-handed?"

He shrugged. "It's my boat. Are you going to cooperate or not?" Placing one hand behind her, he trapped her against the chart table. "If you don't like the way I handle things—" his voice was husky, his face very close to hers "—I can always drop you off at another of the islands."

Her green eyes blazed. He wouldn't get rid of her that easily. Not with his overbearing attitude or his sneaky brand of sexual harassment. "Shall we get on with it?" she suggested politely.

He laughed softly and moved away. "This," he said, indicating a small stove and sink, "is the galley."

Rachel clenched her fists at his tone. He sounded as though he were taking a group of school children on a tour. *Can you spell galley?*

"Pete or I will show you how to use the equipment tomorrow. You'll be expected to take your turn with the meals. This bunk is Pete's." Moving forward to another bunk, he said, "This will be yours for the trip. The bolster is a sleeping bag. If you need help with it, ask Pete."

"I think I can probably manage," she said, gritting her teeth.

Directly across from her bunk was a dining booth. He leaned his hand on the folding table. "The dining alcove makes a berth...which is mine. The head is there, and I'll assign you a locker tomorrow. We use fresh water only when absolutely necessary. Keep your personal things out of the way, and remain fully clothed at all times."

"You mean if I have this giant urge to shuck my clothes I can forget it?" she said, staring at him innocently.

"That's right," he said, as though her question had been a serious one. Leaning back against the wall lazily, he said, "The main thing you have to remember is that this is not Boston. On the *Nightingale*, I'm the boss. If we need help, you'll help without question." He met her eyes. "You've just paid for the privilege of working your butt off."

"Is all this supposed to put me off? Am I supposed to shudder and say, 'Please, Mr. Flynn, sir, take me back to Atuona'?" She raised her chin. "Boston or the South Pacific, I *always* pull my own weight."

He smiled slowly. "Then we won't have any problem, will we?" He turned and moved past her. "I'm going topside. I suggest you get some sleep—you'll need it."

Suppressing the urge to throw something at him, Rachel turned and unzipped the bolster, shaking out the lightweight sleeping bag. She had to tell herself over and over that it didn't matter—Flynn didn't matter. All she required of him was that he get her to Cleve. But when she finally fell asleep her dreams were of mutiny.

The next morning Rachel stood on the bowsprit, laughing at a group of bottlenose dolphins who had been escorting the boat for several miles. Behind her, sitting cross-legged on the polished teak deck, Pete tinkered with an unidentifiable piece of machinery.

When the dolphins disappeared she made her way back to sit beside him, smiling at his unnautical attire. A white western hat and black jogging shorts didn't exactly shout "South Pacific." Flynn, standing behind them at the wheel, wore an ancient, stained captain's cap and cutoff jeans that rested low on his lean hips.

She glanced down at her blue Pucci shorts and shirt. Somehow they seemed a little touristy in comparison.

"I'm sorry I locked you in the bathroom last night," she said.

"The head," Pete corrected automatically. "Don't worry about it. You caught us fair and square."

She stared at him, her expression bewildered. "And that's all there is to it? Tit for tat? You steal my money and I threaten you with a gun, so now we're even."

"That's about the size of it."

She shook her head doubtfully. "It may take me a while to get used to business practices in this part of the world."

Leaning her chin on her knees, she stared at his amused face. Both men puzzled her. They seemed intelligent, even highly educated. What were they doing drifting around in the back of beyond with—from what she could determine—neither purpose nor occupation?

"Don't you ever miss the United States?"

He glanced up. "Sometimes I wake up from a dream and I miss it like crazy. It's always the same dream and always brings the same overwhelming urge to go home."

"What's the dream about?"

"A Big Mac and one of those chocolate cupcakes that have the white goo in the middle."

She laughed. "You're crazy."

"Probably," he conceded as he tightened a screw. "But one of these days I'm going to fly back for a couple of days and fill up on anything with additives."

Leaning back, she stared out at the ocean. Blue skies, blue water—it was enough to confuse the senses. "It's all so beautiful...but how do the two of you exist out here without jobs?"

"We have jobs. Flynn rents out the *Nightingale*, and we both crew for rich tourists...like you. We're not living in the lap of luxury, but we do okay."

"If you're doing so well, why does Flynn owe everyone in Atuona?"

"You exaggerate," he said, his black eyes sparkling with laughter. "He has a few debts. So do I. But everyone knows that we're good for the money."

She gave him a skeptical glance. "What about the men who were after Flynn last night? They evidently weren't so sure they would get paid."

"That's different. That wasn't a legitimate debt—at least, that's not what started all the ruckus. Those men were part of Joe Teahitue's family—uncles, cousins and assorted in-laws. Some of them may have lent Flynn money, but they wouldn't have tried to collect like that if it hadn't been for Joe's wife."

Rachel frowned. She should have known a woman was involved somehow. "What did Joe's wife have to do with it?"

He grinned. "She's had the hots for Flynn since she first laid eyes on him. Somehow Joe got the idea Flynn was making it with her. He started suggesting strongly that Flynn pay him for the privilege. When Flynn told him he was crazy, Joe got a little testy. He got all his relatives together and came hunting for Flynn. They were either going to get paid or perform group surgery."

She was silent for a moment. "Was he . . . 'making it' with Joe's wife?"

Pete shrugged. "Who knows? That's Flynn's business."

"But it affects you," she said logically. "You can't ever go back to Hiva Oa."

"They'll calm down," he said, unconcerned. "They always do. Joe's old lady will start chasing someone else, and a new feud will be on."

She leaned back against the rail and stared at him. "You seem so sane. How did you ever get involved with someone like Flynn?"

"My choice. Flynn may get me into trouble occasionally—" He glanced up and grinned. "Okay, frequently. But he never fails to get me out again. And it works both ways. I've had a few close calls due to my own stupidity—too many. There was a delectable little sweetheart on Fatu Hiva who turned out to be a chief's daughter. Her old man nearly started a war over that. If Flynn hadn't been there to rescue me, right now I would either be bare bones on the bottom of the ocean or married with a dozen kids.''

When Pete talked about Flynn there was not only affection in his voice, there was respect. Rachel was more confused than ever. ''How did you get together originally? Did you grow up together?''

He shook his head. ''I grew up in Kansas. My mother was a Marquesan who married an American sailor she met in Tahiti. Mom turned into an all-American, feet-on-solid-ground citizen of Kansas. But she must have given me a few stray genes. Even when I was little I heard the sea in the wheat fields and smelled saltwater in old man Morgan's pond.'' He laid the shiny piece of machinery aside and leaned back against the rail, his arms behind his head. ''So after college I decided to see the world. I made it as far as Hong Kong . . . and that's where I met Flynn.''

He gave a low chuckle, as though the memory amused him. ''That was six years ago. We've been together off and on ever since.''

Rachel stared straight ahead at the open ocean. Did she have a friend she could stand to spend six years with—work and play? She didn't think so. She had been too busy trying to prove to Asa that she was as sharp in business as any man . . . as sharp as a son would have been. She had always avoided close relationships, male and female. She had Cleve and Asa and her work. They were all she needed.

''Now it's your turn.''

When Pete's voice interrupted her thoughts, she brought her gaze back to him. ''My turn?''

"Questions and answers. What are you doing in the South Pacific, and why would you choose the Alexandras, of all places, to visit?"

"I didn't choose them," she said, smiling. "They chose me. I'm here for my brother's birthday."

He shook his head in amazement. "They must be right when they say the rich are different. It seems a long way to come for a birthday party. But I suppose socialites don't have schedules to keep."

"What is it with you two?" she asked in exasperation. "I admit my father has money. So do I. But what money I have, I made on my own. Work. Maybe it's not something Flynn is too familiar with, but it's how I pay my way in the world. I no longer live with my father in Boston. I have an apartment in Manhattan. Right now I have a project underway in Massachusetts—a hotel-shopping complex—that will make news all over the country. No professional dilettante could have accomplished that."

"Okay, okay," he said, laughing as he held up a hand, as though to ward off her anger. "No need to get hot under the collar. Maybe we misjudged you, but be fair. If you can automatically assume we're bums, we can automatically assume you're a socialite."

She smiled ruefully. "Point taken," she said.

"So which island is your brother on?"

"That's the problem," she said, frowning. "I don't have a clue. I only know it's one of the Alexandras. He's there with a cult."

Pete whistled softly. "Son of a gun. Old French Polynesia is making progress if we've got a genuine cult. Your brother's a little strange, is he?"

She smiled. "No, just a little lost. When our mother and his father—Cleve is my half-brother—were killed in a car accident last year, Cleve seemed to be suddenly cut adrift. He had nothing solid to hold on to. That's how he got involved in this thing. He was wide open for the promises Bruce made—a new and better world—all the usual things."

"Bruce?" Pete asked in disbelief. "A guru named Bruce? Now I've heard everything."

She grinned. "Yes, I know it sounds odd. But whatever his name, he seemed to have all the answers for Cleve. I suppose these people always do. Cleve thought he could find what he was looking for with him."

"What was he looking for?"

She shook her head. "I don't know...peace, maybe. And since he couldn't find it inside himself, he's trying to find it through outside sources." She frowned. "I've only got a week to find him. Since he was six, I've spent every one of his birthdays with him, even when Asa threw fits. I'm not going to miss this one."

"Asa?"

"My father," she said.

"I take it your father and stepbrother don't get along too well."

"That's what's so exasperating. Asa's never even met Cleve, but he hates him because he's a constant reminder that Mother preferred someone else." She glanced up. "Don't get the wrong idea. Asa's a good man, but he's proud and stubborn. I suppose he needed both those qualities to get where he is. His father was a carpenter."

"Didn't hurt Jesus much."

"Jesus didn't live in Boston," she said dryly. "People can judge you by some pretty strange values. Coming from a background of poverty, Asa has always felt that he had to prove he was better than everyone else. He worked his way up to where he is— one of the wealthiest, most influential men in Massachusetts. When he finally made it, he married my mother, a genuine Boston deb." She inhaled slowly. "She left when I was five and married Matthew Harcourt, a prominent state senator. I saw them together occasionally, and I'm convinced they loved each other. But Asa thinks she left him because he was beneath her socially. That's why he was so determined that I become top socialite of the year and prove the McNaughts are as good as anyone else."

"Did you? Become a socialite, I mean."

She shrugged. "For a while, just to please him. But I already knew I wouldn't fit in. There's too much of Asa in me. It drove me crazy spending day after day attending luncheons and fashion shows and charity balls. I needed a purpose." She laughed softly. "It took me a long time to convince Asa that high society was simply not my *metier*. That's another reason he resents Cleve. My brother is accepted by all the 'best people' as one of their own."

"Not too many of the 'best people' join a cult and run away to the South Pacific."

"No, they don't," she conceded. "But Cleve will find himself eventually. I'm sure of it. All he needs—"

She broke off and jerked her head around when she heard a loud crash. Pete was on his feet instantly, moving nimbly toward the back of the boat.

"One of the fuel drums is loose," Flynn shouted from the cockpit. "Come on, Boston, hop to it. We need every hand. Help him secure it again."

Rachel frowned, then moved toward Pete. The maverick drum rolled wildly with the pitch of the boat, knocking Rachel and Pete off their feet more than once, but at last they managed to get it into position and tie it down.

Afterward Rachel went below to clean up. She looked at her right hand and moaned.

"What's wrong?"

Rachel glanced up as Flynn entered the cabin. Pete had evidently taken his place at the wheel. She shoved her hand behind her back. "Nothing."

"Don't be stupid. Let me see." Reaching behind her, he pulled her hand toward him and examined the back, then turned it over to look at the palm. "I don't see anything... except a couple of broken nails."

"*Three* broken nails," she said stiffly. "But I'm not complaining."

"Don't get testy. Did I say you were complaining?" He flopped down on her bunk. "You've got to learn to loosen up, Boston."

She bit back a caustic retort. It probably wouldn't have done any good anyway. Flynn seemed to be asleep. After a moment she went into the head to wash her face.

She was hot and dirty and exhausted. But, although she would never admit it to Flynn, she was somehow content. Living on a boat was a crude sort of existence, but there was something compelling about the vast expanse of ocean around them. The isolation was complete; no piece of the civilized world intruded here.

Moving to the open companionway, she paused. It was odd, but the phrase "civilized world" almost had the ring of an insult. What was wrong with her?

When she felt a hand on her shoulder, her elbow went back in an automatic reaction. Flynn grunted loudly and rubbed his stomach. "Where the hell did you learn to do that?" he asked warily.

"The seventh grade," she said, making no apology.

"You must have had an interesting childhood," he muttered wryly. "I wasn't trying to attack you. I merely wanted to know if you're still brooding about your nails."

"I never brood," she said stiffly.

"Pout, sulk, mope—whatever you want to call it." He picked up her hand and briefly kissed each finger. "Now, is that better?"

She jerked her hand away. "I don't care if all my nails fall off. It's not important." She glanced away from him. "And I want you to stop...that."

"That? What?" he asked, his eyes wide with mock innocence.

"You know very well what," she said. "Stop doing intimate things like kissing my hand. I hired you to find my brother...that's all."

He reached out and wrapped his hand around her neck, his thumb caressing her militant chin. "Things getting too hot for you?"

She met his eyes, her gaze stubborn. "I can handle anything you can dish out, Flynn." She reached up and tugged at his hand, trying to remove it from her neck. "But I will not have you manhandling me."

He turned his hand and captured hers without effort. Leaning close, he met her gaze squarely. "Manhandling?" he said softly. "Boston, when and if I decide to manhandle you, you can bet a few bossy words won't stop me." Then, before she could do much more than sputter in fury, he was gone.

Swinging around, Rachel kicked her bunk violently. Back in Boston she had no problem handling a whole crew of rough workers. But one idiot in a smelly captain's cap infuriated her to the point of helplessness.

Staring at the companionway, she decided she would simply stay out of his way as much as possible. That wasn't admitting defeat, she assured herself. It was simply a matter of using good strategy. If she avoided him, he couldn't goad her into losing her temper.

Even though the *Nightingale* was relatively small, she managed to stick to her plan for the rest of the day. When there were no more run-ins with Flynn, Rachel at first felt smug. Then, gradually, she began to realize that he hadn't even noticed that she was avoiding him.

Thick-headed pig, she thought, her features disgruntled as she watched the sun dip into the water that evening. Pete had gone below to sleep, leaving them alone, but now that there was no reason to avoid Flynn, Rachel stayed topside. He probably wouldn't notice that, either.

Suddenly she gave a soft laugh. How Asa would love seeing her like this. It hurt her father's chauvinistic, masculine pride that so often she was stronger than the men she worked with.

But then, she thought ruefully, none of those men had been Flynn.

She turned her head slightly to look at him where he stood at the wheel. His tanned flesh gleamed from the light of the thousand stars behind and above him. Shadows made his face harsh and intense, a sharp contrast to what she had come to know of him.

"You know," she said quietly, "I can understand how once you were here you would want to stay. But what drove you to come here in the first place?"

There was a long moment of silence before he spoke. "You're looking for a mystery...all women love mysteries. But this time you're way off base. I'm not running from anything, and there's no grand philosophical answer to my presence here. I'm not searching for the meaning of life, or any such garbage. The reason I'm here is because this is where I want to be...simple and boring."

Even with this spectacular display of stars, Rachel couldn't see his expression, but somehow she knew there was more to Flynn than he would let on and, although she hated to admit it, he intrigued her.

She stayed for a while on deck, but made no other attempts at conversation. Then, yawning wearily, she stood and made her way below, leaving the puzzle of Flynn for another day.

Flynn heard Rachel as she left; then her movements were lost in the sounds of the sea. He shook his head slightly at the memories her question had brought back. It wasn't good to remember too much of the past. It was better to get on with the present. But sometimes, like tonight, the past refused to be ignored.

He would never forget the first time he had seen his boat. She had been lying on her side, ready for the scrap yard. He had merely shaken his head and walked on. A few minutes later he was back, staring at the shape that was more junk than boat. Paint was peeling off in ugly chunks, but he could just make out the name. *Nightingale.*

It was almost laughable—a Cinderella name for an ugly stepsister boat. But Flynn didn't laugh. For a long time he stood beside the boat. The name pulled at his imagination. Someone had wanted to fly around the world on the wings of a nightingale. Had they ever made it?

When he left the docks that day it was with the ownership papers in his pocket. All the way back to

Manhattan and throughout the next week he told himself that he was crazy to throw good money away on a leaky old tub like that. But the next weekend he headed back to Long Island and the *Nightingale*.

It took many such weekends before he even knew if the boat would ever be seaworthy. The renovation was a long, slow process, one that he stubbornly refused to hand over to someone else. Every step he did alone—refinishing the deck and hull, refurnishing the cabin, new parts for the motor, sturdy new sails.

And as the *Nightingale* became more and more the boat she had been, Flynn became less and less the man he had been. An obsession was growing. Even at work he dreamed of finally being able to take her out to open sea.

And after a while the thought of a short trip wasn't enough. He had put too much into her to be satisfied with that. He knew now that the *Nightingale* had been built to last a century. Her last owner had mistreated her, then dumped her. She deserved better than that. She deserved the grandeur of that world tour. And so did Flynn.

By late spring he had arranged to take a year off. He would finally get all this sailing business out of his system once and for all.

Early one summer morning Flynn left Long Island. Before he had been gone a whole day he knew he had been foolhardy to make the trip alone. Although he was an experienced sailor, handling the boat took every bit of his energy. But he refused to give it up. He had come too far to back out at the last minute. So he sailed on—down the east coast, around Florida and through the Panama Canal to the Pacific.

There were times in the next few weeks when Flynn was sure he was going to die alone in the middle of the ocean. And there were times when he was too exhausted to even care. He fought storms and doldrums, sun and wind and rain. And still he kept going.

By the time he reached Hawaii he was no longer the same man who had left Long Island. He had survived. He was tougher and surer and stronger. And he knew he could never go back to New York.

Being alone for that length of time had given him an abundance of time to think. Slowly he began to see that the man he had been in New York was someone he didn't want to know, much less be. He was exactly like all his friends, too friendly faces hiding too grasping thoughts. He had been caught up in the frenzy to get to the top, the frenzy to mate with as many women as possible, the frenzy to put one over on his business associates.

And, like a reformed alcoholic who can never take another drink, Flynn knew if he went back it would start all over again. Sooner or later he would be back in the same old frantic rut. He might have been able to maintain his objectivity if he had had a wife and family to keep him on an even keel. But Flynn had no one but himself.

When he left Hawaii, heading for Tahiti, he had made his decision. After the trip he would settle in Texas or Nebraska, anywhere that was sane. But New York was out.

Several days later, for a reason he would never fully understand, Flynn decided to skip Tahiti and head straight for Hong Kong. Perhaps because he had mentally said goodbye to a fast-paced city, he needed to visit another to check his response.

He needn't have worried. Victoria was exotic, but underneath it was the same as New York. He kept away from the flashy hotels and restaurants, heading instead for the Wanchai district east of central Victoria. Tenements, colorful street markets and most of all, people, crowded every available inch. Flynn felt that his lonely struggles with the ocean had given him the right to mingle with these people who fought daily for their lives.

It was in a Wanchai bar that he had met Pete. Actually, Pete hadn't exactly been in the bar; three men were forcibly helping him out of it. He had come flying through the door with them at his heels, each one determined to do imaginative and lasting damage.

Flynn hadn't liked the odds and had stepped in to even them up. An hour later they left the district in a hurry, battered and bruised, but firm friends. They took in the pleasures of Kowloon together, finding that their dissimilar lives had led them to similar conclusions.

When he learned that Pete was headed for the Marquesas to see where his mother had spent her childhood, Flynn offered the *Nightingale* as transportation. They could take in Tahiti on the way.

All this had taken place a long time ago, but Flynn would never forget his first glimpse of the Marquesas. The islands hadn't smiled their hello, they had shouted it at the top of their lungs. Their very existence was emphatic.

It was here that Flynn shut off the memories. He never allowed his thoughts to go past this point, telling himself it was useless to keep dragging up the pain like an old bone. All the memories were in the past; getting Rachel McNaught to her brother was the present.

Chapter Six

Rachel sat cross-legged on the deck as she cleaned salt from the binoculars. Glancing up, she laughed as Pete shinnied up the main mast like a monkey.

They had been at sea for two days, but for Rachel time had lost its substance. It was as though an entire world, an entire reality, was contained on the *Nightingale*. The relationship between her and Flynn hadn't changed; he still goaded her to the point of murder. But the bickering seemed normal now. She accepted it just as she accepted the easy camaraderie offered her by Pete.

"Land ho!"

Shading her eyes with her hand, she peered up at Pete. "Are you teasing me again?" she shouted to him.

"Would I do that?" he asked coyly. "Look for yourself."

Standing, she raised the binoculars and aimed them in the direction he had indicated. She saw only low clouds. Searching carefully, she finally found an indistinct gray mass floating above the horizon. Was this truly an island? Minutes later the mass solidified, then turned into a sharp green spire of land that pierced the clouds.

"Flynn!" she said, excitement filling her voice as she made her way unsteadily to the cockpit. "Is it Kamahele?"

He didn't take his eyes from the horizon. "That's it," he said quietly. "Our first port of call."

Within an hour they were sliding past lush jungle. Coconut palms came right to the edge of the water, shading the passing boat. As soon as they entered the small bay, islanders dove into the water and swam out to meet the boat, laughing and calling out to the three aboard.

The island's dock was little more than loose boards thrown on pilings. Children, as surefooted as mountain goats, swarmed across, never noticing the missing planks. Their colorful tapa cloth *pareus* covered them—boys and girls alike—only at the hips and upper thighs. In sharp contrast to their clothing, one boy carried a portable tape player, the music blaring.

"Stevie Wonder?" Rachel asked in surprise.

"You were expecting the Tasaday with stone age tools?" Flynn asked, grinning down at her. "Music reaches every corner of the world, places where religion and ideology can't even get a foothold.''

When he began staring at something beyond her, Rachel followed his gaze. Making his way along the beach toward them was a man in Bermuda shorts, a loose white shirt and a huge straw hat.

"Reverend Scudarri," Flynn said from behind Rachel.

With the enthusiastic help of the children, they climbed across the rickety dock to meet him. "It's good to see you again," Flynn said, extending his hand.

"Have I met you?" the reverend asked, peering through thick glasses. "Yes, of course I have. You're—"

"Flynn," he said. "And this is Rachel McNaught, and my friend Pete."

"Company!" the old man said, slapping his hand against his thigh. "What a rare treat. Come, come. You must join me for a drink at my house and tell me why you're here. No, Grace," he said in French to a chubby little girl, "you can't come this time. I'll bring our visitors to the village later to meet your parents."

Without waiting for their consent he turned and walked the way he had come, calling out to the children in Polynesian. Flynn, Rachel and Pete followed him along the trail that led into the thick jungle. The reverend hummed as he walked, giving the impression that he had completely forgotten their presence.

Rachel glanced at Flynn. "You said he was a *little* batty? I feel like Gretel following the witch to the gingerbread house. Maybe we should leave a trail of bread crumbs.''

Flynn merely laughed, but Pete whispered, ''You got that right. The man's nutty as a fruitcake. Positively gives me the willies.''

A short distance into the forest they suddenly came upon a large egg-shaped clearing. At the narrow end a small, raised house sat alone. Beyond it they could see the red roof of a church. Several goats and pigs ran loose around the house, and chickens roosted on the porch railing.

The Reverend paused for a moment on the sagging porch, then swung around to face them, staring in narrow-eyed bewilderment. Then his face cleared and he said ''Guests!'' before opening the door.

The reverend's house consisted of one room. An iron bed stood against the wall, and a wooden table and two wooden chairs filled the middle of the room. The only civilizing touch was a large bookcase filled with books.

''Please, sit down, all of you.'' He waved his arm around. ''Make yourselves at home.''

Pete glanced around the room, shrugged and flopped down on the floor. Rachel and Flynn took the chairs at the table.

''Gracious me, it's nice to have visitors,'' Scudarri said as he poured straight gin into green plastic cups. Turning around, he paused to stare at Flynn. ''Haven't I seen you somewhere before?''

''In Atuona,'' Flynn reminded him patiently.

"No... no, I don't think so," he murmured as he handed round the drinks. "Wait—Atuona. Yes, of course, Atuona." He smiled at Rachel. "You're very pretty. Wouldn't you like a drink, dear?"

She glanced down at the cup in her hand, but before she could think of anything to say he had moved away to sit on the bed.

"Now, what were we talking about?" he asked with smiling enthusiasm. "Oh yes, Atuona. I don't get to the Marquesas often. The last time must have been... let's see..."

"Two years ago," Flynn said.

"Two years ago," he finished, as though the thought had just occurred to him. "So many people." He shook his head. "It's confusing for an old man." When he moved the bed creaked in complaint. "I much prefer Kamahele—although since Tioti became chief it gets a little hectic now and then. Still, they're good children. Yes, they're wonderful children." His voice faded, and he seemed to drift away from them into the world of his own thoughts.

Taking a hefty gulp of gin, Flynn grimaced and set the cup on the table. "Reverend Scudarri?"

"Yes?" He glanced up with a startled look that Rachel was beginning to think was habitual.

"You've lived here a long time," Flynn said. "I guess you know the Alexandras pretty well."

The reverend nodded. "As well as any outsider can."

"Have you heard of a cult recently being established on one of the islands?"

"Cult? No, no—you have it all wrong. Not in the Polynesian islands." He paused, his expression thoughtful. "Now in parts of Melanesia there is a kind of religion called a cargo cult. They believe that someday a giant cargo ship will bring them a share of the goods Westerners enjoy. But here..." He shook his head. "We have no cults."

"Reverend," Flynn said, smiling to conceal his impatience. "I don't mean—"

"I will admit," the reverend interrupted, "that Takaroa, the older god, and Tane, his son, are still remembered by the people. But only as a myth. My children are good Christians." He frowned. "I can't get them away from the idea that a supernatural force, *mana*, flows through certain objects and people. If they think something has too much *mana* it becomes taboo, and they won't go near it."

"But the other islands?"

Scudarri rubbed the loose flesh on his chin thoughtfully. "I'm afraid all the Alexandrans stick pretty much to their own islands. Occasionally we'll have visiting fishermen from one of the other islands, but not often." His eyes clouded, and he cocked his head as though listening to something. "Lately," he murmured, "there has been something in the wind, things told only in whispers."

"What kind of things?"

"Even after thirty years they don't quite trust me. Thirty years," he repeated vaguely, then glanced at Flynn. "You must meet Tioti, the new chief, while you're here. He's young and reckless, but he's a good boy." He chuckled, rocking forward slightly. "I remember when he was just a child. He was so eager to learn. I taught all the other children their lessons, but most of them couldn't even grasp the basics of the French language. Tioti was different. He needed more. The missionary fund—we're nondenominational, you know—helped with correspondence courses, and then there was that Frenchman..." His eyes focused on the wall, as though he were seeing the past. "That's probably where it all started." He shook his head. "Anthropologists are a pagan lot. He put all those ideas in Tioti's head, then left him on his own with those books. A boy with his imagination just had to build stories. That's where his theory came from."

Flynn glanced at Rachel and shrugged. Pete rolled his eyes, then downed his drink in one swallow. Standing, he moved close to Flynn and whispered, "I'm going to check on the boat and make sure his 'children' aren't disassembling it." He turned his eyes toward the reverend and muttered, "Nutty as a fruitcake," then walked out.

"The theory is ridiculous, of course," Scudarri said, completely unaware of them. "But Tioti is stubborn and, after all, it does no harm."

"What theory, reverend?" Rachel asked gently.

"What?" He blinked as though coming awake. Then he smiled. "You're very pretty, my dear. I haven't seen golden hair in years."

"What is Tioti's theory?" she prompted.

"Oh, you've heard about his theory?" he asked, smiling in surprise. "You mustn't put too much stock in it. He's more or less creating fairy tales when he says that he and all Polynesians are descended from the Incas."

Rachel and Flynn exchanged glances. "That's ... interesting," Rachel said.

"Perhaps. But hardly possible. This fellow Heyerdahl put forth the theory years ago, but the bulk of the evidence doesn't support it. I've tried to explain this to Tioti, but he's stubborn." He sat up straighter. "Now you mustn't think I worry about the rituals. They're harmless ... just children's games. And they always come to church on Sunday morning. That means something, doesn't it?"

"I'm sure they value you and your church," Rachel said, her voice soothing.

"Exactly," he said in satisfaction. "All my children are very religious." He glanced around at his visitors. "Would you like to see the church? We're sinfully proud of it."

"That would be nice," Flynn said. "But we'd like to talk to the islanders first. Why don't we save the church until last?" When he shot a meaningful glance at Rachel, they both stood to leave.

"Tioti!" Reverend Scudarri said, looking beyond them at the door. "Come in and meet our visitors."

An arresting young Polynesian entered the room. He had the face of a desert Arab, a lion's mane of black hair, and stood well over six feet tall. On him, the traditional *pareu* looked regal. There was an air of authority about the way he carried himself.

"This is Tioti, the new chief," Scudarri said. "Tioti, I'd like you to meet Flynn and...I'm sorry, my dear, I seem to have forgotten your name."

"Rachel," she said, smiling politely at the newcomer.

"We're pleased to meet you, Tioti," Flynn said.

"The pleasure is mine, I assure you," Tioti said. His accent was strongly French, but his English was beautiful. And even as he spoke to Flynn, he stared at Rachel. "This woman is yours?"

Rachel frowned at the flash of amusement in Flynn's eyes. "No," Flynn said, his voice too serious to believe. "Miss McNaught is a type you wouldn't recognize. She belongs to no one but herself."

As Flynn talked to Tioti about the other islands Rachel shifted in discomfort. Although the chief politely answered Flynn's questions—giving him no meaningful information—he never took his eyes from Rachel. A few minutes later he turned and abruptly left the room.

Later still, as they followed Reverend Scudarri to the village, Rachel and Flynn spoke in low voices. "This place is very strange," Rachel said. "The reverend is strange...the way he refers to all these people as his children. I know that's not unusual, but when he says it—as Pete says, it gives me the willies."

"Take a good look at some of them," Flynn said, his voice dry. "He probably has a right to call them that."

"Flynn! He's a minister."

"That doesn't keep him from being a man." He paused, glancing down at her. "And speaking of being a man, I think Tioti was smitten."

She shivered. "What was with him? I expected him to check my teeth any minute."

"Are you interested in botany?" the reverend called back to them.

They picked up their pace, catching up with Scudarri as he began to tell them about the island's plants.

"Now, this is one you won't find in the United States."

He stooped beside a bushy plant. It looked innocuous, but when the reverend turned over one of the hand-shaped leaves, small red thorns were visible.

"This is the *faufau*," he said. "As far as I know it grows nowhere in the world other than the Alexandras. If one of the thorns puncture the flesh, it's lethal."

Rachel took a cautious step backward, causing the reverend to glance up. "You're right to be worried, my dear. One little scratch on the arm and the flesh would begin to swell. If no antidote is given, amputation would be the only way to save your life."

"But there is an antidote?" she asked.

He smiled. "We are standing in the world's largest pharmacy." Moving forward a few steps, he said, "You see this plant with the tiny purple flowers? This is the *teiroo*. If you get a *faufau* scratch, you simply steep the flowers of the *teiroo* like tea and drink the liquid. In about twelve hours, you're as right as rain. The only side effect is a heavy, sometimes violent delirium." He chuckled. "But who would mind a little mania to save one's life?"

He moved on to another plant, but this time Rachel watched from a distance. Her interest in botany was decreasing by the minute. She had no wish to run into any of the reverend's exotic flora.

As they approached the village they saw that Pete had arrived before them. He stood by one of the bamboo huts, the sides of which were rolled up to catch the breeze. He was talking to the children who had met the *Nightingale*. Tioti was also in the village, surrounded by a group of his people. When Rachel and Flynn drew nearer silence fell, and the Kamahele islanders turned to watch them approach. One of the women broke away from the others and stepped up close to Rachel and Flynn. Reaching out, she tentatively touched Rachel's blond hair, making an admiring sound.

Reverend Scudarri spoke in Polynesian to one of the men, then turned to Rachel and Flynn. "They asked if you would be their guests for lunch."

As soon as they consented, Rachel, Flynn and Pete were ushered into the largest of the huts, evidently a kind of meeting hall. Following the reverend's example, they sat on the floor on woven mats.

Immediately women began bringing in food in polished wooden bowls. Sea urchins, raw fish soaked in lemon juice, lobster, algae cooked in coconut milk, roasted bananas, piles of fresh papaya, oranges and mangos—after two days of canned beef stew it was a feast.

Flynn and Pete seemed completely at home, but it took Rachel a while to unwind. She carefully copied the manners of the islanders around her, but drew the line at sticking her fingers into the large communal *popoi* bowl that held the fermented breadfruit mash.

After the meal they all filed out of the hut. Several of the women and children gathered around Rachel. They didn't touch her, but simply stood and stared, talking to each other in excited whispers. Rachel smiled until her lips hurt, glancing around frantically for help from Flynn and Pete.

She saw the two men standing in the open area at the middle of the village. One of the younger islanders approached, then whispered something in Pete's ear while pointing toward the surrounding jungle. Seconds later Flynn and Pete joined a group of men, and all of them headed toward the forest. Several giggling women followed behind.

Reverend Scudarri followed her gaze and chuckled. "Veo must have brought a jug of the local white lightning."

"And you approve?" she asked incredulously.

"It's all harmless fun. They'll go off into the jungle and have a party, then tomorrow they'll all have headaches."

One of the children edged closer to Rachel, who smiled at the little girl, then turned to Scudarri. "Why do they stare at me so intently?"

"It's your hair, my dear. There's a local legend about a goddess with golden hair. When she appears there will be a royal wedding and all the evil of the earth will disappear." He nodded toward her hair. "They consider you royalty because you have the same color hair as their long-awaited goddess." He shrugged. "As I said, the old gods are still remembered, but it's perfectly harmless."

Let Flynn have a party in the jungle, she thought, raising her chin. At least he wasn't royalty.

Glancing around, she found that the reverend had quietly disappeared. She struggled to remove herself from her cloak of children and walked toward the path that led back to the bay. Immediately Tioti approached her.

"There will be a ceremony at the *paepae* tonight, *mademoiselle*," he said quietly. "We would be pleased to have you attend as our guest of honor."

Rachel glanced around. What was she supposed to do now? She had seen the stone platforms—the *paepae*—on the Marquesan islands. They were somber places, alive with the echoes of pagan rituals. But would she offend custom if she declined the invitation?

Since all her advisors had deserted her, Rachel had no choice but to accept. "Thank you, Tioti. I would be pleased to be your guest."

He nodded shortly, then clapped his hands. Immediately Rachel was being pulled toward the jungle by a group of laughing women.

"Wait," she said, finding their laughter contagious. "Where are we going?"

They merely giggled at her and guided her deeper into the jungle. They passed a vast stone platform, which Rachel assumed was the setting for tonight's celebration. At one end stood an ancient, carved stone figure. Rachel had no chance to examine it, because her escorts were still pulling her along enthusiastically.

Suddenly the jungle stopped at the edge of a crystal-clear stream. A canopy of green covered it, letting in golden shafts of sunlight. It was a fairy-tale place that took Rachel's breath away.

"It's absolutely beaut—" She broke off when the women began pulling at her clothes. "What are you doing? Stop that!" she said, slapping at their fingers.

When they dropped their hands Rachel backed away from them, then paused when she saw their hurt expressions. "All right, all right," she muttered. "Don't sulk. You want me to take a bath, I'll take a bath." She began to remove her blouse. "But I can undress by myself."

The women giggled and, against her continuing protests, helped her take off her clothes. Each garment was examined thoroughly, the filmy bra and panties causing excitement as well as amusement.

"I don't like bathing in front of an audience," she complained as she stepped into the water, knowing they didn't understand a word. "We don't do this kind of thing in the United States . . . at least, we don't do it in Boston."

Two of the women shed their clothes and followed her into the water. When they began scrubbing her skin with sand Rachel protested again. "Listen—listen to me," she said, shrugging them away. "I don't need your help. I can do this—" she made a rubbing motion on her arm "—myself." Again she saw the confused hurt. "Oh hell," she said in defeat. "You win. One of you can wash my back—but only my back," she added quickly, pointing to her back.

Some minutes later, when she stepped from the stream, they rubbed the water from her body with scented flowers. Rachel merely stared at the trees and endured their attention, knowing they wouldn't understand her embarrassment.

At that moment a young woman Rachel had not seen before came through the foliage, carefully carrying a white dress. Cut low at the neckline, it had puffed sleeves and a long, slim skirt that belled out at the back in a demitrain. It was obviously intended to be her royal raiment, and after some minor adjustments—made on the spot by what Rachel assumed was the local seamstress—the dress fit beautifully.

"I take it underwear is not *de rigueur*," she murmured, her voice dry as she smoothed the tight skirt over her hips.

They placed a crown of white flowers on her head. Then, still giggling, the whole group escorted her away from the stream.

"I feel so ridiculous," Rachel murmured to the trees. "When Flynn and Pete see me, they will absolutely split their sides laughing. How did I—"

She broke off as they reached the *paepae*. This time the women didn't seem to mind when she stopped to stare. The stone tiki was a stout demon with giant, round eyes and a wide grinning mouth. His hands rested on a protruding belly. Placed before the statue was a wide slab of rock, sculpted into a turtle. It looked like a throne . . . or an altar.

As they walked on the girl who had brought the dress smiled at Rachel and said shyly, "You are lucky. You are the first to be chosen."

"You speak English," Rachel said, her expression showing her surprise.

"Yes, Tioti teaches me," she said, dipping her head modestly.

"That's very kind of him."

"Yes, he is a good man," she said with innocent pride. "He does not have to waste his much-needed time with me, the last of his wives."

"You're his wife?" She was surprised. The girl couldn't have been more than fourteen or fifteen.

"I am Lahia, his third wife. Liliuohe and Iolani were his wives before me."

"He's been widowed twice?" It didn't sound too healthy for wives in this part of the world.

"Widowed?"

"His other wives died," Rachel explained.

Lahia shook her head in soft-eyed confusion. "No, they live in the chief's house with us. We have ten children. I have given birth to only one, but I'm new. Iolani says I will catch up."

Rachel bit her lip. She knew it was illegal for him to have more than one wife, but she didn't want to upset this sweet girl. "Lahia, what did you mean when you said I was the first to be chosen?"

"To be Inti's bride," she said enthusiastically. "It is a great honor. Even greater than being Tioti's bride. You see Inti is not only a Kamahele god, he is also an Incan god, the god of the sun. Tioti has told me all about him. Many years ago Inti came across much water to find—"

"Wait a minute," Rachel said in confusion. "Tioti didn't say anything about this. He just said I would be the guest of honor."

"Yes, great honor," the girl assured her earnestly. "Inti has been waiting many years for his bride with golden hair. If you are the true one, peace and prosperity will come to Kamahele."

Rachel stopped abruptly just as they broke through the foliage into the village. "I've changed my mind," she said, smiling politely. "I think I'd better find my friends. You see—" she began to back away "—I can't possibly get married without them being here."

Lifting her skirt, she turned to run. "It's been very nice, but—"

She broke off when she ran straight into Tioti. He gave a sharp order in his own language, and two men appeared out of nowhere to grasp Rachel's arms.

"This is ludicrous! Stop it! Let go. *Flynn!*" she shouted as they dragged her, kicking and screaming, into a small hut.

The two men easily overcame her struggles. Holding her still, they used slender grass ropes to tie her hands to the support posts. When they had finished they left her alone without a word.

Rachel breathed deeply and slowly, her face flushed, her dress torn. "Damn you, Flynn," she said. "Where are you when I need you?"

"Yeeee-ha!" Pete yelled, stomping his feet enthusiastically as he watched the cockfight.

Flynn shook his head and took another drink from the gourd. The alcoholic substance he and Pete had been given by the islanders was just now beginning to go down easily. It was about 170 proof and, if he survived, would probably leave him cross-eyed.

All afternoon the men had kept his and Pete's gourds full. Flynn had poured most of his on the bushes behind him. He didn't want to offend anyone, but the stuff was lethal. Pete, with his hollow leg, had been drinking as freely as the other men. No amount of alcohol seemed to affect him.

Flynn glanced up when Pete disappeared into the jungle with one of the giggling women. Alcohol wasn't the only thing Pete could never get enough of.

When he felt a gentle touch on his arm, Flynn smiled down at the voluptuous woman beside him and shook his head in regret. "I'm sorry, sweetheart," he said in rusty Polynesian. "Not this time."

How long had they been gone from the village? he wondered. It seemed only a short time, but already shadows were stretching out across the small clearing. He needed to get back and see how Rachel was getting along.

He chuckled softly. She was probably conducting a woman's lib seminar. Either that or she would be as mad as fire at having been left alone.

Flynn hadn't been enthusiastic about having a tropical party, but he'd known he needed time away from her to unwind. The two days on the *Nightingale* had given him a lot to think about. He had expected her presence to be an intrusion. He had been wrong. She fit in as though she had always been with them.

He frowned. That wasn't good. He couldn't get used to her presence. She was a job—extra money to pay his debts. When they found her brother, she would go back to her hotels and shopping malls and men with capped teeth who played golf with hand-balanced clubs.

And then things would get back to normal, he assured himself silently. In a few weeks he wouldn't even remember her name.

Throwing aside the gourd with a strangely violent movement, Flynn rose to his feet and began walking in the direction of the village.

Rachel's arms ached. It was getting dark in the hut. Outside she could hear the villagers making preparations for the ceremony.

"Flynn, you low-life bastard," she said aloud.

"For a Boston blue-blood you certainly use some salty language."

Rachel jerked her head up. The voice had come from the window. "Flynn? Is that you?" she whispered.

"Who else?" he said. "What in hell are you doing now, Boston? Introducing the natives to S&M? When a couple of the islanders tried to keep me away from the village, I figured something was up." He paused. "You sure get into some interesting situations."

"You...you...just get me out of here," she said between her teeth. "This is all your fault. I wouldn't be in this 'interesting situation' if you hadn't left me alone with these savages while you went off to fill up on rotten papaya juice and—yum-yum!"

He laughed softly. "Settle down and tell me what's going on."

"I'm tied to these posts," she said tightly. "What more do you need to know?"

"Did you insult someone? I knew your smart mouth would get you in trouble sooner or later." When she sputtered in indignation he said, "Temper, temper. I suppose this is why they were trying to get me and Pete drunk."

"I wouldn't think that would take much effort on their part," she said caustically. "It was probably to keep you from interrupting the barbecue...because evidently I'm the main course."

"Don't be silly. They don't practice cannibalism anymore."

"So why am I tied up, Flynn? Is this one of their charming local customs?"

"Didn't they say anything before they tied you up?"

"Sure, they said I was royalty. These are the royal ropes on my hands. Then Lahia—Tioti's wife—said I had been chosen to be a bride for their god. Not just an average Polynesian god, you understand—a genuine Incan god. Only the best for Rachel McNaught." She moaned. "They're probably going to throw me in a volcano."

"There aren't any volcanoes around here," he said, chuckling softly. "And that's a Polynesian custom, anyway. You've got an Incan god. I think the Incas cut the living heart out of their sacrificial victims."

"Oh, well that makes all the difference," she said, her voice cutting. "It doesn't matter if they drown me in chocolate mousse, dying is dying! Get me out of here!"

"Shh. Let me think a minute."

The silence seemed to go on forever, then he said, "I don't really think this is as serious as it seems. This is the twentieth century. However provoking, Boston socialites are just not sacrificial material. They'll probably dance around you for a while, then let you go, but—"

"Probably?" she interrupted, her voice high-pitched with incredulity. "And if you're wrong you'll say, 'Oops, my mistake,' while I become a heart donor."

"But just in case," he said, as though she hadn't spoken, "I'd better get you out."

"Brilliant conclusion. I could have told you that five minutes ago." She inhaled, forcing her pulse to slow. "What are you going to do?"

"We've got to get rid of the men guarding the hut."

"That's good," she said eagerly. "How do we do that?"

"We provide a distraction."

"Of course, a distraction."

"I'll go back to the boat and get some bullets. I'll throw them in the fire, and when the guards run to see what's happening, I'll come in and untie you."

"That might just work. In fact, I think it's a wonderful idea," she said in relief.

"Okay, hang tight—sorry, no pun intended. I'll be back in about half an hour."

She didn't hear him leave, but she immediately felt his absence. The minutes stretched endlessly as she waited. Flynn could handle it, she told herself bracingly. He had sounded too confident to fail. Then suddenly she heard the loud cracks as the bullets exploded. Her heart began to pound. The plan was working.

Five minutes later two men carried Flynn into the room and, with remarkable efficiency, drove four stakes into the dirt floor and tied his hands and feet to the stakes, then left without even acknowledging Rachel's presence.

Flynn moaned, then suddenly jerked his head up and looked around the room. When he saw Rachel, he closed his eyes and let his head sag back to the floor.

"That was a really lousy idea, Flynn," she said slowly.

"Critics I don't need," he muttered. "It's a little hard to be inconspicuous in a place where all the men run around in their BVD's."

"So now what do we do?" She paused, then said warily, "How do you feel about being the best man at my wedding?"

Without warning Reverend Scudarri walked into the hut. "Where are they?" he murmured vaguely. "I know I left them somewhere."

He glanced around the small hut, his gaze sweeping over Rachel and Flynn as though they weren't there.

"Reverend!" Rachel said in relief. "We're so glad to see you."

"Yes? What?" His eyes seemed to focus at last as he stared at her. "Hello, my dear. You look very pretty. I've misplaced my glasses...again." He shook his head. "I can't prepare my lessons without them."

"Scudarri," Flynn said slowly, "untie us."

"If only I hadn't sat on my extra pair," he said as he moved toward the door to leave.

"Reverend!"

He glanced over his shoulder. "So nice of you to humor the children." He chuckled. "They do like their games." And then he was gone.

"Damn!"

"You addlepated old fool!" Rachel yelled after him. "He should be defrocked or whatever they do to nondenominational missionaries. These people might as well have the Cheshire cat teaching them."

"Shut up for a minute so I can think."

"Your thinking is what got you where you are now," she muttered, twisting her hands to try to ease the tension. The ropes were beginning to cut into her wrists.

"Since neither of us can reach the knife in my pocket, the only thing we can do is wait for them to untie us, then try to make a break. Pete is our ace in the hole. He'll come looking for us sooner or later." He frowned, remembering the woman Pete had taken into the jungle. "Maybe later." He ran his gaze over her. "By the way, I like your dress...especially the strategically placed rip in the bodice."

Rachel knew that half her breasts were exposed, but there was nothing she could do about it. She leaned her head against the wall. "Keep your eyes to yourself."

"You know, Boston, there's something very provocative about the contrast between the suggested innocence of the white dress and your hands tied above your head like that," he said as though Rachel hadn't spoken. "Vaguely orgiastic and very fetching."

"Flynn...shut up." She glanced down at him. "You don't look fetching. You look like a fool."

She had lied. The way he was spread out, with his arms stretched tight, every muscle was exposed. His neck bulged with the effort of keeping his head up. His chest, smooth and shining with perspiration, looked massive. The muscles of his abdomen were pulled in with the strain of holding his awkward position, leaving the waist of his shorts looser than usual.

Her eyes dropped below the waist and a choking sound caught in her throat at his obvious condition. She jerked her head up, meeting his eyes.

He smiled and shook his head. "I told you—there's not a damn thing I can do about it."

"You barbarian," she said, closing her ears to his laughter.

Then suddenly her eyes grew wide. "Oh, Flynn." The words were barely a whisper as she watched Tioti walk into the hut. Across his shoulders hung a floor-length cape covered with thousands of tiny brilliantly colored feathers. His crown was also made of feathers and stood twelve inches high.

Flynn, hearing her stunned whisper, raised his head in time to see four men follow Tioti into the hut. "It's party time," Flynn said as two of the men began to untie him.

Tioti watched for a moment, uttered a sharp command in Polynesian, then left as abruptly as he had appeared. When two of the men began to untie Rachel's hands she kicked out at them, but her foot became entangled in the wide demitrain.

"Don't struggle, Rachel," Flynn said. "This is what we want."

The men pulled them into the jungle along the same trail Rachel and the women had taken earlier that day. They heard music and chanting that grew louder as they neared the stone platform.

"Flynn," she said warily, "I don't like this. I hate blood—it always makes me dizzy."

Flynn laughed deep in his throat. He had to give her credit. The socialite wasn't going to get hysterical.

As the six of them climbed the wide stone steps leading to the *paepae* they were scarcely noticed. Blazing torches illuminated the islanders, who danced in the center of the platform. Gourds were being passed around freely, the alcohol contributing to the frenzy of the dancers.

Rachel stared, feeling her heart jerk in rhythm to the drums. Then she caught her breath. Through the wildly gyrating bodies she saw Pete, dancing just as feverishly as the others, and just as drunk.

"Our ace in the hole?" she called to Flynn above the noise.

"I saw him. Don't worry...just keep quiet and be ready to move."

At that moment Pete looked up and caught Flynn's eye. Flynn nodded slightly. Rachel glanced back and forth between the two of them, wondering what the gesture meant. Then Pete abruptly stopped dancing. Leaning his head back, he howled like a wounded coyote and grabbed Lahia by the arm. The shy girl cried out in terror as Pete tried to pull her into the jungle that grew thickly behind the stone platform.

Tioti, standing beside the stone god, swung around. When he saw his young wife being dragged away he let out a violent roar that stopped the music and dancing instantly. Every head turned toward him, waiting in frozen silence for their chief's wrath to fall.

The feathered cape flapped as he walked toward Pete and the girl. Before he reached them, Pete began to speak in Polynesian, pointing to a man standing nearby.

The man shook his head feverishly, saying, "*Aoe...aoe,*" the Polynesian word for no.

When Tioti continued to stare at him, the young man turned and swung at Pete, catching him a glancing blow on the shoulder. Tioti called out to two men. They moved forward, trying to hold the young man Pete had accused.

He fought them wildly, kicking out at Tioti. Three other men protested his treatment and tried to pull Tioti's men away. Within seconds most of the men and some of the women had joined the fracas, some swinging according to their affiliations, some simply because they enjoyed a free-for-all.

The two men guarding Rachel whooped and left to join the fight. One of those who was guarding Flynn took a step away, then glanced back in indecision. Without warning Flynn clasped his hands together and brought his fists down on the neck of the man closest to him.

When the one who had been moving away turned toward Flynn, Rachel yelled, "Flynn, watch out." She tried to hit the Polynesian, but tripped and fell awkwardly to her knees.

Flynn swung around, his foot flying out to kick the man in a place that doubled him over in agony.

"Last one to the *Nightingale* is a rotten egg," Pete said, grinning broadly as he jumped over Rachel and ran down the stone steps.

Flynn pulled Rachel to her feet, and they began to run. On her way down the steps the train of the white dress became tangled around her ankles. Barely pausing, she pulled it up around her thighs and kept going.

A crashing in the underbrush behind them told them that their departure hadn't gone unnoticed. As they ran through the dark jungle Rachel tried not to think of what would happen to them if they were caught. She merely followed Flynn. Her lungs felt on fire as they ran across the beach to the rickety dock.

Pete was on the *Nightingale*, ready to cast off, when Flynn and Rachel jumped the rail at last.

Rachel sank to the deck in exhaustion, curling up to stay out of the men's way. Within seconds they were underway and safe from harm. She watched the angry islanders on the beach disappear behind them as the *Nightingale* headed out to open sea.

Chapter Seven

What do you mean, my fault?" Rachel stood on the deck, her hands on her hips as she stared at Flynn in belligerent disbelief. "This is your territory. You're supposed to know these people. If you hadn't been out in the jungle partying everything would have been fine."

"If you hadn't decided to play queen for a day none of this would have happened," he said, towering above her. "You hired me to get you to your brother, not to be abstinent. Pete and I refrain from drinking while we're underway—that's just good sense. But when we're ashore our time is our own." He frowned, dropping his gaze to the white dress. "And for heaven's sake, fix that dress. You're hanging out of it."

Pulling the remnants of the bodice over her breasts, Rachel raised her chin and stepped past him. "I should know better than to try to communicate honestly with an uncouth, uncivilized egomaniac. I'm going to bed."

It was difficult to remain dignified and walk against the steady rocking of the boat, but somehow she managed. When she passed Pete at the wheel he was laughing.

"Oh, shut up," she muttered as she went below.

After grabbing her nightclothes out of her locker, she went to the head to change. When she came out the lights were out. And although she couldn't see him, she knew that Flynn had come down also.

Carefully keeping her eyes away from his berth, she unfolded the sleeping bag and spread it out on her bunk. When the boat slipped sideways she took several halting steps backward and fell heavily on top of Flynn.

"You're just naturally attracted to my bed, aren't you?" He chuckled huskily as his arms came up to steady her. Instead of gripping her waist or her arms, his fingers were spread suggestively across her buttocks.

"Don't you wish," she said. She had intended the words to be sarcastic, but they sounded breathless to her own ears.

When she pushed against his chest he slowly removed his hands, and Rachel moved back to the other side of the cabin. She cautiously climbed into the sleeping bag, keeping one foot on the floor until she was sure the boat wasn't going to throw her on top of him again.

Lying stiffly on her back, she stared at the darkness above her. She was exhausted, but her mind was too active to allow her to sleep.

"Boston?" The word was a soft whisper.

She clenched her fists but murmured casually, "Hmm?"

"I concede that we were both at fault."

"That's big of you," she said dryly.

"It isn't polite to get snotty when someone offers an apology," he said, his voice mildly scolding.

"Is that what that was?" When he didn't reply she bit her lip. "All right," she said reluctantly, "I admit I got carried away and got myself into trouble... and I accept your apology." She paused, then drew in a breath. "I forgot to thank you and Pete for getting me out of that mess. You handled yourselves very well."

"You're not too shabby in a pinch yourself."

She felt the tension seep out of her. She smiled in the darkness, turning toward him slightly. Maybe Flynn wasn't so bad after all. When he made the effort there was a rough kind of charm about him that some women might be drawn to... not her, though, she hurriedly assured herself. But she was woman enough to appreciate what other women might see in him.

"For a socialite," he added, with amusement filling his voice.

Rachel gritted her teeth in annoyance. She should have known. Any goodwill she was feeling toward him disappeared immediately. Rolling sharply onto her side so that she no longer faced him, she pulled the pillow over her ears to block out the sound of his soft laughter.

Rachel stared at the stove, biting her lip. In the quietness of the cabin she could hear the soft roar of the auxiliary engine. The wind had died several hours earlier, making the sails impotent.

Today it was Rachel's turn to prepare lunch. When it had been her turn before, she had served sandwiches. But they hadn't obtained fresh supplies on Kamahele, as they had intended, and it was difficult to fix sandwiches when there was no bread.

Leaning against the counter, she sighed heavily in self-pity. Pete had shown her how to use the stove the first day out, but somehow all his instructions had gone out of her head. She could just see the look of amused condescension Flynn would give her if she went up to ask for help.

Raising her chin in determination, she started to work. If she blew up the boat it would be Flynn's fault.

The first time the engine sputtered Rachel barely noticed, so intent was she on what she was doing. The second time it sputtered was more obvious because it didn't catch again. The boat wasn't moving.

She listened to the silence for a moment, then stepped up into the companionway. No one was at the wheel. "What's wrong?" she asked.

"It's the engine," Pete called down to her.

"I gathered that," she muttered under her breath. "Can you fix it?"

"We can give it a good try."

By the time they came below to wash up the engine was still silent, and the hot meal she had prepared was cold. The two men didn't even seem to notice as they sat down to eat.

"We're not far from Mana Kula," Flynn said as he ate. "The wind is picking up. It's from the wrong direction, but if we tack we should be able to make it in a couple of hours."

Pete nodded. "Let's just hope they have a carburetor that'll work. I don't like being underway without the auxiliary."

"We're that close to the next island?" Rachel asked eagerly. Surely on this one they would find news of Cleve.

Flynn cut his eyes toward her. "We're that close. This time try to stay out of trouble."

Her eyes blazed, but before she could explode he stood and moved toward the stairs. "Okay, let's raise the sails."

Because the wind died several times it was closer to three hours before they sighted the next of the Alexandras. From a distance they could see a small town close to the bay. And anchored in the small harbor was a large, sleek yacht, flying, along with the French courtesy flag, an American flag.

"People," Rachel said as she waved to two women on the deck of the yacht. "Real people."

"So what are we?" Pete asked. "Termites?"

Flynn chuckled. "I don't think you want her to answer that question."

She swung around to face them, her eyes shining. "No, really, you've both been terrific." In her excitement she was willing to forget all their differences. "But it'll be nice to talk to someone from home." She paused. "I wonder if they've visited any of the other islands. Maybe they've even seen Cleve."

"Don't get your hopes up," Flynn warned. "Why don't you check them out while Pete and I try to scrounge up that carburetor? We can ask the villagers about the other islands later."

"That's a wonderful idea." She headed for the companionway. "I've got to change into something decent."

Pete glanced down at his shorts, then looked at Flynn. "Do you suppose khaki is still in? Maybe we'd better change, too."

"Your gold lamé would look nice," Flynn said thoughtfully. "It goes so well with canvas shoes."

As Rachel left them she grinned, for once not minding their teasing. She was too excited about seeing other Americans.

While she was cleaning up she heard them securing the boat to the small wooden dock. Then they left to go ashore. She was arranging her hair when she heard someone shout.

Going topside, she found that a man and the two women she had seen earlier had rowed over to the *Nightingale*. "Hello," Rachel said, leaning over the handrail.

"I'm Deidre Marshall," a pretty redhead said. "And this is Audrey Boyd, my aunt. And at the helm of this grand vessel is my Uncle George." She indicated the two older people in the boat with her. "We've come to invite you all back to the *Fianna* for cocktails. Like you, we've only just arrived and thought it would be nice to have company." She grinned. "We're terribly bored with each other."

"Is it cocktail hour already?" Rachel asked, returning the woman's smile.

Audrey laughed. "Haven't you noticed that it's always cocktail hour in the tropics?"

"I suppose you're right," Rachel said. "My friends have gone ashore, but I'd love to come."

"Wonderful! George, give her a hand."

Deidre talked constantly on the way to the yacht, evidently relieved to have someone more her own age to gossip with.

After a tour of the elegant yacht Rachel reclined in a lounge chair on the deck with the others, drinking something with a little pineapple juice and a lot of gin.

"This is wonderful," she murmured politely. "How long have you been out?"

"We left San Francisco sometime in May." Deidre lay on a mat beside Rachel. She wore a tiny white bikini and was golden brown from the sun. "I can't even remember what month it is. All the days seem to have run together."

Rachel laughed. "I know what you mean. It's a strange experience." She paused. "San Francisco—is that where you live?"

"My aunt and uncle live there. I'm from San Diego."

Rachel turned to Audrey, who was sitting in a deck chair nearby. Her taciturn husband was somewhere below. "You don't happen to know the Spellmans, do you?"

"Jean and Charles?" Audrey asked. When Rachel nodded the older woman's hazel eyes sparkled with excitement. "Do you really know the Spellmans? What a small world. Ohh, how unoriginal. But isn't it wonderful? What are you doing here? Is that your boat?"

Rachel shook her head. "No, I hired it on Hiva Oa. I'm touring the Alexandras. Have you been to any of the other islands?"

"The other Alexandran islands? No, this is the only one we'll see." She glanced toward the shore. "It seems awfully primitive. We're on our way to the Marquesas, then back to Hawaii."

Deidre sat up. "Aunt Audrey, I've just had the most marvelous idea." She glanced up at Rachel. "Why don't you send your boat back to Hiva Oa and come with us?"

"Oh yes, do," Audrey urged. "We've plenty of room. Deidre and I have completely run out of things to say to each other. We leave for Nuku Hiva early tomorrow morning and plan to spend several days there. It'll be such fun having you along."

As Rachel smilingly declined their invitation she was overcome by the oddest sensation. She had been so excited about seeing "civilized" people again. Deidre and the Boyds were very nice. But now that she had met them, she felt that she didn't belong with them. She was anxious to get back to Pete and Flynn and the little boat that had no designer furniture and no designer people.

As soon as Flynn and Pete walked into the store that was the main structure in the village, a short, stout man appeared from behind a faded curtain.

"Hello, welcome to Mana Kula," the man said enthusiastically, his French accent overpowering. "I am Jean-Paul Jusserand. How can I help you?"

While Pete gave the Frenchman the specifics of the part they were looking for, Flynn glanced around the large room. It seemed to be a combination general store and bar-and-grill. Several tables with candles in the center were set up to the left of the large room, and on the right a duke's mixture of grocery and hardware items was piled on tables and shelves.

"Oui," the Frenchman was saying to Pete, nodding his head as he spoke. "I'm sure I have it here somewhere. I'll look." He started to poke through boxes and into cubbyholes. "The organization is not so much, but I will find it. You'll see."

"Have you lived here long, Jean-Paul?" Flynn asked, leaning against the counter.

"For ten years." He laughed heartily. "I came on vacation and forgot to leave."

"Do you know the other islands?"

He shrugged, his eyes narrowing as he stared at Flynn. "Some I do, some I don't. Why do you ask?"

"We're looking for newcomers—a cult—that's recently moved onto one of the islands. Have you heard of such a thing?"

The Frenchman didn't speak for a moment. Then, dropping a part back into a box, he moved back to the counter. He wasn't smiling any longer.

"I have heard nothing," he said stiffly. "I am sorry, but it seems I don't have the carburetor after all."

Pete stared at him for a moment. "Wait a minute, Jack," he said, leaning across the counter to grab his collar and pull him close. "What are you trying to pull? We didn't fall off the tater wagon yesterday, you know. You said you had the part. Now, where is it?"

Very carefully Flynn loosened Pete's grip on the other man. Shaking his head ruefully, he smiled at Jean-Paul. "Sometimes he has fits. We beg your pardon."

"*Qui est* 'Jack'?" the man asked in confusion. "*Qu'est ce* 'tater wagon'?"

Flynn shrugged, still smiling as he said, "Thanks for your help. Come on, Pete."

Outside Pete said quietly, "We know he was lying, and he knows we know he was lying. But *why* was he lying?"

Flynn frowned, glancing back at the store where Jean-Paul stood in the doorway watching them. "He was not only lying about the carburetor, he was lying about the cult. Did you see him stiffen when I asked about it?"

"Maybe one of his kids ran off and joined."

"Maybe," Flynn said doubtfully. "But somehow I don't think so."

"Flynn! Pete!"

Flynn turned to see Rachel and what he supposed was the group from the yacht walking toward them.

"The Boyds have invited us all for dinner on their yacht," Rachel said after she had introduced them all.

"That sounds like a winner to me," Pete said, grinning. "It's my turn to cook tonight."

If Rachel had expected Flynn and Pete to be out of place with the luxury on board the *Fianna*, she was mistaken. They were just as much at home on the sleek yacht as they had been in the Kamahele hut. The Boyds welcomed the two men graciously, asking them polite questions about the *Nightingale* and their life in Atuona.

It didn't take Rachel long to see that Deidre had fallen for Flynn like a ton of bricks. After dinner the two of them stood at the rail, the redhead in her Dior gown, Flynn in his denim cutoffs.

Flynn didn't look a bit uncomfortable. In fact, he looked cute, Rachel thought in disgust. Swallowing her drink, she turned back to catch what Audrey was saying. "Your friend Pete tells us there's a bar in the village. Why don't we move the party ashore? I love these primitive spots."

When everyone agreed to move they rowed ashore. On the beach Flynn managed to shed Deidre long enough to drop back beside Rachel. "I think we may have found a clue," he said softly.

"From Deidre?" she asked incredulously, her mind still on the redhead.

He stared at her in confusion, then said, "In the village. Where's your mind?"

"I'm sorry." She shook her head to clear it. "What did you find out?"

"Nothing really substantial, but the man who runs the store, and the bar we're headed for now, acted very strange when I asked him about a cult. He suddenly refused to sell us a carburetor."

"What are you going to do?"

He shrugged. "Unless you want us to beat the information out of him, there's not much we *can* do. But if he knows, maybe someone else on the island does, too. We'll just have to start questioning people tomorrow."

At that moment Deidre reclaimed Flynn, making conversation impossible. Inside the bar the party sat at a large table in the corner of the room and ordered drinks. After a while Pete left them to join some islanders at another table.

And the whole time Jean-Paul didn't take his eyes off Flynn and Pete.

Rachel studied the stout Frenchman, resenting him even though she had never met him. According to Cleve, Bruce was unrelenting in guarding the privacy of the cult. Could he have paid Jean-Paul to divert people from their island? Maybe if she explained why they were looking for the cult, that she had no wish to disrupt things but merely wanted to see her brother, he would be more open.

At that moment Pete, with a woman on each arm, approached the table. "If you need me, I'll be at Lihuane's place. Turn at the second palm tree on the left. It's the house with the big hibiscus in front."

As she watched them leave the bar Rachel raised a slender brow and glanced at Flynn. "Two?" she asked.

He shrugged. "It's the age of specialization."

Rachel followed his gaze back to Jean-Paul. The Frenchman stood behind the counter, talking to two Polynesian men. The men nodded several times as Jean-Paul spoke with them quietly. When the Frenchman turned his head and met Rachel's eyes she glanced away quickly and resumed her conversation with the Boyds.

Several minutes later the two Polynesian men casually walked by their table, jostling Flynn as they passed. Flynn glanced up, looked them over, then turned back to his companions.

Mr. Boyd frowned, but kept his silence until one of the men shouted something in Polynesian. "What's he saying?" the older man asked.

"I didn't catch all of it," Flynn said lazily. "But I think it was something about clumsy, stupid Americans."

The laconic Mr. Boyd was either intensely patriotic or had imbibed too freely. He stood abruptly and faced the two men. "You, sir, are the one who is clumsy. You ran into Mr. Flynn, then had the gall to blame him. And, as for stupidity, at least Americans learn to speak a civilized language."

In the course of his speech George had moved to stand chest to chest with one of the men. Raising his hand, the Polynesian pushed the older man away. It was enough for George to think he had been attacked, and when he regained his balance he swung wildly at the Polynesian.

"Flynn," Rachel said urgently. "He's going to get hurt."

"I don't think so," he said, smiling. "Look."

When Rachel turned back to the argument Audrey was scolding the bewildered Polynesian vehemently, tapping his massive chest sharply with one finger as she spoke. Deidre stood behind her, urging her aunt on.

Rachel gave a startled laugh and turned back to Flynn, to find him walking away. She stood and caught up with him. "Where are you going?"

"Jean-Paul just left. I'm going to follow him," he said, his voice low. "You stay here with the others."

Rachel made no protest. She merely waited a few seconds, then followed him. Outside the bar she stopped for a moment to let her eyes adjust to the darkness. The voices from inside were muffled, sounding almost as soft as the warm tropical air.

She glanced around quickly for Flynn, then froze when she felt a hand on her shoulder.

"Somehow I knew you wouldn't stay put," Flynn whispered in resignation.

"I have as much right as you to know what's going on. More. My brother is involved." She looked up at him. "Where did he go?"

"That house over there." He indicated a house on stilts near the bay. Other than the fact that it was isolated, it was exactly like the other houses in the village.

"Hadn't we better get closer?" she asked. "It's going to be a little hard to keep an eye on him from here."

He glanced down at her and frowned. "Okay, I'll allow you to come along, but stay behind me and keep your mouth shut."

"Allow me?" she asked, her eyes blazing. "You'll allow me?"

Rolling his eyes in exasperation, he grabbed her hand and pulled her toward the house. He avoided the front, moving to the side where a light shone from the window. Staying flat against the outside wall, he cautiously peered inside.

Rachel bit her lip in frustration. She couldn't see a thing. Stooping, she crossed to the other side of the window before Flynn could stop her.

Inside, Jean-Paul sat at a radio set. He had on heavy old-fashioned earphones and spoke in rapid French for quite a while. Then he paused to listen.

After a moment he spoke again. "No," he said, his voice nervous. "I've never seen them before. Yes, two men. They are asking questions. What shall I do?"

He paused again. "But how? How do I stop them?" In the ensuing silence he closed his eyes, a pained expression on his face. "Do you mean—but I can't." He inhaled deeply and nodded. "*Oui, je comprends.* I will stop them."

He flicked off the set and leaned his head against it. Flynn beckoned to Rachel, and together they moved away from the house.

"'By the pricking of my thumbs, something wicked this way comes,'" Flynn murmured when they were several yards away.

Rachel was still trying to take in the mysterious conversation. "Do you think he has instructions to kill us?"

"Not us," Flynn said. "Just me and Pete. He thinks you're with the Boyds . . . and we'll keep it that way. Come on, let's find Pete."

Following Pete's directions, they found the house with the hibiscus in front. "Pete's not going to like this," Flynn said, chuckling, then he knocked softly on the door and walked in.

Rachel stared out toward the bay, shifting uncomfortably when she heard the women giggling and squealing.

"Your timing leaves a lot to be desired," she heard Pete say when the door opened again. "Good evening, Rachel," he said with dignity as he moved past her, adjusting his clothes as he walked.

When the three of them arrived at the bay they saw the Boyds and Deidre being rowed back to the yacht.

Suddenly Flynn stopped walking and held up a warning hand. Startled, Rachel followed his gaze. In the moonlight they could see two men on the dock, leaving the *Nightingale*. They were the two men who had started the argument in the bar.

When the men had disappeared into the night Flynn and Pete went aboard, leaving Rachel alone on the dock.

"All right, you can come aboard now," Flynn called to her from the cabin.

On entering, she found them staring at a small contraption on the table. It consisted mainly of a glass jug and a timer. "Is that . . . is it . . . ?"

"This is an uneducated guess you understand," Pete said, nodding. "But I would say it's definitely a bomb."

She gasped. "A bomb? That's crazy. What's going on? Who told Jean-Paul to stop us . . . and why?"

Flynn stood, his face uncharacteristically serious as he carried the bomb to the deck and tossed it overboard. "Let's get away from here, then we'll talk."

The wind was working for them now, and two hours later, when the island had disappeared into the ocean behind them, Flynn told Pete to drop anchor.

Both men stared at Rachel as they entered the cabin. She frowned. "Why are you looking at me like that?"

Flynn sat at the table, leaning on his forearms. "When you explained that you wanted to find your brother, you gave the impression that it was pretty straightforward. What did you leave out?"

"You think I expected this kind of trouble?" she asked in disbelief. "If I acted like it was a straightforward thing it was because I thought it was just that. I want to find my brother—"

"To wish him happy birthday," Pete finished for her.

She pushed back her hair. "All right, I admit that sounds strange...but I've explained the situation to you, Pete. Cleve's birthday is important to me." She inhaled slowly. "And I just want to make sure he's happy. That's all there is to it."

"And you have no idea why someone would want to keep us away from the island where your brother is?" Flynn asked quietly.

"Not like that." She leaned back wearily. "Look, I knew this man Bruce didn't want strangers around. Since Cleve told him that he had no family, I knew it would be a little awkward when his sister showed up. I decided to handle that problem when I got there. But I never dreamed getting there would be dangerous."

"Why did your brother say he had no family?" Flynn asked, studying her face.

"It was one of the requirements for joining. He said Bruce didn't want trouble with deprogrammers." She shook her head. "I didn't like it, but legally he's an adult. I couldn't have stopped him—not that I would have tried. He's always been too much in his father's shadow. He needed to find out who he was. I thought he would spend a few months out here—maybe even a year—then come to terms with himself."

She glanced up. "He said they didn't use drugs or any kind of brainwashing. They were simply a group of people who wanted to live in peace away from the terrors of the modern world." She shrugged helplessly "I thought it sounded harmless."

"You were wrong," Pete said flatly.

"We can't know that yet," Flynn said. "This may have nothing to do with the group the boy joined. We gave Jean-Paul the idea that we were going to check all the islands. We don't know who he was talking to."

"Whoever it was has influence," Pete said. "The shopkeeper didn't look the type to embrace a cause. He must be on someone's payroll."

"What does all this mean?" Rachel asked urgently. "What has Cleve gotten himself into? Is he in any danger?"

"That depends," Flynn said, rising to his feet. "Your brother may know what's going on, may in fact be a part of it."

Rising slowly, she faced him. "You're wrong," she said, her voice low with anger. "Not only would Cleve never hurt me, he would never hurt anyone. If you knew him you would know how ridiculous the suggestion is."

"Well, I don't know him, do I?" Flynn said. "I wasn't trying to insult your brother. I just wanted you to know that everything is speculation until we find him." He moved away from her. "And we won't do that in the next few hours, so let's all get some sleep."

How could she possibly sleep? Rachel wondered in agitation. All this time she had thought Cleve was safe and happy. She had pictured him helping the others plant a garden or whatever it was they did in communes. She had thought he would be working out his problems in peaceful surroundings.

Abruptly she said, "I think I'll go topside for a while. I need some air."

When Flynn joined her, she was sitting on the deck, her arms wrapped around her knees as she stared out at the dark, silver-streaked water.

"Stop worrying," he said. The words weren't sympathetic; they were more in the form of an order. "There's nothing you can do until we find him."

She nodded, keeping her gaze on the horizon.

"Come on, Boston." His voice softened as he sat beside her. "You can't lose your grit now. Stop imagining horror stories. He's probably sitting in the middle of a bunch of teeny-boppers discussing the decadence of the capitalist system."

"Why didn't I check this thing out?" Her voice was quiet and intense. "I could have hired a dozen private investigators to make sure it was on the up and up. Why didn't I?"

He shrugged. "Maybe you didn't want to take away his dignity. Maybe you wanted him to know that you believed in him and his judgment."

She sighed, relaxing slightly. "Yes, you're right. That's exactly why I didn't. But I'm beginning to think Asa has the right idea. Manipulation is looking more attractive every minute."

"Your father is working from a different base," he said, his voice thoughtful. "He's had to be in control every minute to get where he is."

She turned her head toward him, resting it on her knees. "What do you know about Asa?"

"I heard you and Pete talking about him." He leaned back, supporting himself with a forearm on the deck. "And besides, Asa McNaught is not exactly an anonymous figure. You can't read the *Wall Street Journal* without knowing who he is.''

Her eyes widened in surprise. ''You read the *Journal*?''

''I used to.'' His voice was brusque. ''That was a long time ago.''

She stared at him. ''You're a very confusing man, Flynn. I can't figure you out.''

''You're not supposed to. I'm simply the hired man. I do what I'm paid to do.''

''Nothing about you is simple,'' she grumbled. ''On the surface you're an adventurer, not adverse to a little minor larceny now and then. But there's more.'' She shook her head. ''Asa taught me to judge character. For some insane reason I trust you. I have from the beginning. Otherwise I would never have joined you and Pete on the *Nightingale*.''

He was silent for several minutes; then, in a movement that took her completely off guard, he pulled her to the deck, wedging her beneath his body.

''Don't trust me,'' he said, the words low and harsh as he grasped her chin, forcing her to look into his eyes. ''If you expect to find more than a larcenous adventurer you'll be disappointed.''

Lowering his head, he kissed her roughly and deeply, as though he were trying to prove something. Rachel couldn't move, not because he held her so tightly, but because her senses were stunned by the unbelievable force of his kiss.

Drawing back slightly, he stared into her dazed eyes, his features fierce. ''Money isn't all I steal,'' he said as his hand moved up to capture one breast. "Do you still trust me?"

She tried to regulate her uneven breathing, but it was no use. He was pulling emotions and desires out of her that Rachel wasn't even aware she possessed.

When she didn't answer he grasped her shoulders and gave her a violent shake. "Do you?"

Slowly she nodded her head. "Yes," she whispered.

A groan caught deep in his throat as he lowered his head to capture her lips again. The harshness was gone, replaced by a need that seemed as great as Rachel's own. She slid her fingers into his hair, reveling in the sensuous feel of it as she held him close.

For long, heated moments they lay entwined on the smooth deck, rocked gently by the waves, enveloped in the brilliance of a thousand stars. Somewhere, on the edge of her consciousness, Rachel realized that what she was experiencing was more than desire; she had felt desire before, and it in no way matched the emotion that was unfurling inside her. There was a depth and a painful sweetness to it that were lacking in ordinary lust.

Then, before she had a chance to explore what was happening to her, the beautiful interlude was over. Rachel felt Flynn withdraw mentally even before he pulled away from her and rose to his feet.

She lay where she was, uncaring that her blouse hung open and that her hair was spread around her head in tangles. She simply stared up at him in bewilderment.

"Like I said," he rasped out, "don't trust me. Lock away your silver and your honor. I'll steal either one without a second thought."

Turning abruptly, he walked to the companionway and went below.

Rachel's movements were mechanical and awkward as she sat up and straightened her blouse. She was too confused to think, too stunned to feel. She felt trampled.

Distractedly, she recognized the fact that music was coming from the cabin, dark, brooding music. A few minutes later Pete came to sit beside her on the deck.

"I thought you were asleep," she said, her voice still husky with the remnants of desire.

"I was trying, but it was a little difficult with that angel of death blaring in my ear."

"He's a rude pig," she said shortly as the numbness began to disappear.

Pete didn't contradict her. He merely stared up at the stars for a while. "It's hard to be private on a boat," he said quietly. "Sounds and voices carry."

Rachel glanced away from him.

"Look, Rach. I need to tell you something about Flynn. He won't like it, but we're going to be together for a while yet in a very small space. It'll make it easier on all of us if you know where he's coming from." He paused. "Flynn wasn't always this rough a character. When I first met him he was different, more open with his emotions. But he got involved with a girl from Nuku Hiva. He went back to the States to get things settled, and while he was gone, she died." The words chilled Rachel with their starkness. "Since then all his relationships have been casual. I can even see him keeping his distance from me at times. You see, he's afraid now. He's afraid of needing anyone again, so he's convinced himself that he's a loner."

Rachel didn't want to know. She wanted to dislike Flynn intensely. She didn't want to feel stirrings of emotion. "Why are you telling me all this?" she asked tightly.

He shrugged. "Just call it a feeling. Do you hear that music?" She nodded. "He only plays that when he's disturbed about something. You disturb him. I haven't figured out yet if that's good or bad."

He stood up in one fluid motion. "Good night, Rachel."

"Good night, Pete," she said softly, then turned to stare out across the vast, lonely ocean.

Chapter Eight

Douse the canvas!'' Flynn shouted from the cockpit.

Pete and Rachel worked frantically to get the sails down before the wind ripped them to pieces. Rough seas had appeared with no warning an hour earlier, building quickly to violent proportions. They were without power, and now without sails, but the waves carried them faster than either. They could only hope the waves were taking them in the right direction.

To prevent being swept overboard by the crashing waves, they wore harnesses attached to safety lines. Every time the boat dropped in the trough between waves Rachel felt her feet leave the deck and grabbed desperately for something solid.

Again and again waves washed over the side of the boat, drenching everything, pulling at anything that was loose. An unusually powerful wave threw her back against the mast; then, before she could recover, a second fiercer wave struck right behind the first. She was swept off her feet instantly. Grasping the line in terror, she slid across the deck as the receding water pulled her toward the railing.

"Boston!"

She barely heard Flynn's shout as she lay for a second, soaked to the skin, feeling like a fish on a line. Gathering her strength, she pushed tendrils of dripping hair from her face and struggled to her feet.

"I'm okay," she called breathlessly as she pulled herself back to the mast to help Pete.

Half an hour later, as quickly as the sea had become rough, it was smooth again. Without being told Pete lowered the anchor. Rachel unhooked her line and dropped to the deck beside the men, exhausted and wet, but strangely exhilarated.

"You two certainly lead exciting lives," she said, breathing slowly and deeply. "I'm going below to change... any minute now... when I get the strength to stand."

Flynn chuckled. "We only want to give you your money's worth. We've had calm seas since we left Atuona—dull stuff. We couldn't let you go back to Boston without the excitement of almost washing overboard. Right, Pete?"

"Service is our motto," he said lazily.

The tension that had lingered between Rachel and Flynn since the night before had disappeared with the storm. The incident on the deck might have been a dream, she thought, undecided as to whether she was relieved or disappointed.

She sat up. "I'm definitely going below to change. There's something particularly unpleasant about salt water drying on your skin. I feel like I'm being cured for later use."

Thirty minutes later, when she came up on deck again, she felt almost human. The sails were up, and Pete was at the wheel, whistling as though the rough spot had never occurred. Flynn had the binoculars trained on a distant point.

"Land," Pete said, nodding in the same direction. "It's Pohukaina."

Rachel stiffened. She didn't know if she was ready for another of the Alexandras. Would they find mayhem and madness as they had on the other two islands? Or might Pohukaina bring news of Cleve?

"How far?" she asked.

Flynn lowered the glasses. "Half an hour. I can see a village near the beach." He turned to Pete. "I think this time we'll put ashore on the opposite side of the island . . . just in case."

Just in case this was the island where Cleve was, Rachel thought, her eyes clouding. Just in case someone tried again to blow them up. Cleve, she prayed silently, please be safe and happy.

After rounding the small island they anchored the *Nightingale* in a small cove. Because he was part

Polynesian, and therefore less conspicuous if discovered, Pete would scout the area while Rachel and Flynn looked for fresh fruit to supplement their supplies.

As soon as Pete had left the boat Flynn and Rachel waded ashore, carrying a mesh bag for fruit. Parts of the jungle were virtually impenetrable. For unnumbered years trees had fallen, creating a morass of limbs and trunks, piling on top of each other and quickly becoming covered with thick green moss, parasitic ferns and flowers. Interwoven with the rotting debris were live trees and lianas. One wrong step would send an unsuspecting victim crashing through the insubstantial stuff.

Keeping to more congenial areas, they found several different kinds of bananas, including a tiny round variety that tasted vaguely of strawberries. They didn't bother with what Flynn called a horse-banana, since each piece of fruit was as long as one of Rachel's arms. Mangoes, papayas, wild pineapple, oranges, lemons and limes grew all around them. It seemed strange to see white flowers, and green and ripe fruit all growing on the same branches of the citrus trees.

The mesh bag was bulging by the time they started back to the boat. Flynn chuckled at the mango juice dribbling down Rachel's chin.

"I'll have to stop calling you Boston," he said, grinning at her. "You don't look anything like a socialite right now."

"I never was," she said, wiping her mouth with her hand. "I work with my father—at least I try. The hotel-shopping mall complex I'm working on now is the first I've tackled alone."

"A complex. That sounds impressive. But you don't look much like a high-powered executive right now, either. You look more like—"

He broke off when they heard a rustling sound in the surrounding foliage. Holding up a hand in warning, he moved a couple of steps toward the sound, then laughed. "How would you like a luau tonight?"

Moving to stand beside him, she followed his gaze. In the undergrowth a small, bushy Polynesian pig rooted in the dirt. "I don't suppose he's hunting for truffles," she said wistfully, then glanced at Flynn. "I'm torn. Roast pork sounds absolutely ambrosial, but that means we have to kill the poor creature."

"It works best that way," he said, nodding seriously. "Otherwise they squeal when you take a bite."

When the pig moved Flynn made up her mind for her and dove for it. The animal darted away agilely, squealing frantically as he lost himself in thick brush.

Rising to his knees, Flynn began to dust himself off. "Pete should have been here. He's been in a few rodeos in his day." He shrugged. "Oh, well, I guess fresh fruit will have to do after all."

She laughed at his indignant expression. It surprised her to find how much she liked him today. *It's more than liking,* an insidious inner voice suggested, but Rachel refused to listen. It was not a day for thoughts that made her uncomfortable.

"At least I won't feel guilty about that poor little—" She broke off, staring at a deep scratch on his arm. "What did you do to yourself?"

"It's nothing, just a scratch," he said. "I dove into the wrong bush."

She glanced at the foliage behind him, then caught her breath and took a hesitant step forward. "Flynn . . . my God, *Flynn*."

"What's wrong with you?" He stared at her in bewilderment, then followed her gaze to the thorny bush that had snagged him in the arm.

"It's the one Reverend Scudarri showed us," she said, her voice unsteady. "The *faufau*."

He stepped closer to the bush. "No," he said, his tone scoffing. "This is not anything like it . . . is it?"

She nodded. "Look at the leaf. It's shaped just like a hand . . . and it has red thorns." She glanced up at him, her eyes terrified. "It's the same one."

"That crazy old man? You can't trust anything he said. It was probably all a fairy tale." He tried to make the words light and amused, but his eyes didn't quite meet hers.

"You don't believe that." Her voice was tight and strained. "What are we going to do?"

Swinging around, he kicked viciously at a tree. "Damn, damn, damn. This is all we need."

Rachel could almost read his mind. He was angry with himself. He was the man in charge, and although he hadn't been at fault, he was telling himself he had screwed up.

"You can't kick yourself now. We've got to do *something.*" The last word was choked. "Flynn, I can't amputate your arm. I simply can't."

He turned to stare down at her, then suddenly he began to laugh in genuine amusement. "That's good to know," he said, still chuckling. "You keep that attitude, because I have no intention of letting you." He gave her a quick hug. "Thanks for putting things in perspective. What we've got to do now is find that flower that's the antidote."

"Yes—yes, of course," she said in relief. "Do you remember what it looked like?"

He frowned. "No, don't you?"

She bit her lip to keep it from trembling. "I think it was purple with a green tinge to the center... but—"

"No buts," he said, interrupting her. "You're right. I remember it now. Don't start doubting."

She couldn't help it. Doubt ate at her as they began to walk again, neither of them willing to bring up the possibility that she was wrong, or that the flower didn't grow on this particular island.

Although Flynn tried to hide it from her, Rachel sensed when his arm began to bother him. He held it stiffly as they walked. She didn't mention it, nor did she mention the fact that he was tiring. The poison was already beginning to work.

Her gaze darted from side to side, searching frantically for the plant. It had to be here; it simply had to.

"Wait, Flynn—look." Running ahead, she dropped to her knees beside a small flowering plant. "This is it. I'm positive."

She kept her head turned away from him as she felt a quick rush of tears sting her eyes. Dumping some of the fruit out of her bag, she began to pick the small, fleshy blossoms. There were fourteen. Scudarri hadn't given them specifics. She only hoped fourteen would be enough.

By the time they got back on the *Nightingale* Flynn was drenched in perspiration and could barely walk. The flesh around the scratch was swollen and angry-looking. He hadn't spoken for some time. It was as though all his effort had been concentrated on getting back to the boat.

Moving feverishly, Rachel put a pan of water on the stove, then rinsed the flowers and put them in a bowl. When she heard Flynn swear she turned and found him making up his berth.

"Let me do that," she said, moving toward him.

"I'm just fine," he said, his voice brisk and faintly irritable. "You tend to what you're doing."

As soon as the water began to boil she poured it over the blooms. Immediately the flowers and the water around them turned deep purple, almost black.

"How long should I let them steep?"

He shrugged, then winced with the movement. "Just leave them in until the water cools enough to drink." He glanced at the brew. "That stuff looks sickening. I hope that idiot Scudarri knew what he was talking about." He moved to sit down on his berth. "Come sit down, Rachel," he said seriously. "We need to talk."

Rachel winced. He had never called her Rachel; that he should use her name now somehow seemed significant. She sat beside him on the wide berth, gazing up at him in nervous apprehension. Looking vaguely uncomfortable, he stared at the other side of the cabin.

He cleared his throat. "We don't really know what this will do to me. Damn it, Pete should be here," he said vehemently.

"But he's not." The words were quietly spoken. "That means we have to handle it alone."

He nodded reluctantly. "Scudarri said the stuff sends you around the bend. And the whole thing lasts about twelve hours. Pete should be back in three or four hours. I imagine it should be at least that long before the stuff takes effect." He met her eyes squarely. "But just in case, I want you to tie me down, here on my bunk."

"Flynn—"

"I know it's not necessary," he said quickly, smiling as though to reassure her. "But why don't you admit it, you'll enjoy the hell out of subjugating me. Just don't try anything while I'm under the influence," he added cockily.

Shaking her head, she swallowed heavily. "I'm sorry. I can't make jokes about it."

He put his arm around her shoulders and squeezed gently. "Come on, Boston, where's the old militant spirit?"

"I'll do whatever I have to, Flynn," she said, her voice quavering. "I'll do whatever you ask me to do, but I can't pretend that it's nothing, and I can't pretend that I'm not scared to death."

With one hand he pushed her head against his chest. "I won't die on you, Boston . . . you still owe me five hundred dollars."

She laughed brokenly, burying her face in his neck. *I love you so damn much, Flynn.*

The words were only in her head, but they were so strong, so intense, that she felt them in the air between them. The revelation exploded inside her, filling her, dazzling her. It had been coming for days, maybe since that first night in his room, and she had been too blind to see it. She was in love with Flynn.

Standing abruptly, she walked back to the stove. "I think it's cool enough to drink now."

He drew in a deep breath. "Then let's get on with it."

After straining the "tea" into a cup she carefully carried it to him. He stared at the virulent liquid for a moment, then turned the cup over and downed it in one gulp.

He coughed violently, then almost threw the cup at her. "Judas Priest! That stuff would choke a jackal. It tastes like turpentine and dead fish."

She examined his features anxiously. "How do you feel?"

"Nauseated." The reply was short and irritable. "Tie me up, then go do something else. I don't want you standing over me like an elegant vulture." He moaned and rolled back on the bed. "This stuff is not going to stay down."

"Flynn, don't you dare throw up," she ordered, hovering over him. "I'd never find another one of those plants by myself."

He raised his head to glare at her. "I'm not going to throw up. Tie me up like I told you to. There's nylon rope in the locker by the head."

Reluctantly she found the rope and brought it back to the bunk.

"Tie my feet together, then tie my good hand to the hook at the end of the berth. That'll keep me down." He glanced at her. "If it starts before Pete gets back, you stay away from me...and that's an order." Lying back, he closed his eyes.

Even though he couldn't see her, Rachel nodded silently and began to tie his feet. Swearing under her breath, she fumbled awkwardly with the nylon rope.

"Tight, Rachel," he ordered gruffly. "Don't worry if it's comfortable or not."

"I'm trying," she said, jerking on the rope to pull it taut.

He didn't say another word until she had finished. Then opening his eyes slightly, he said, "Now go away."

Biting her lip, she went to the companionway, then glanced back at him. She couldn't simply leave him alone. The arm was already swollen to twice its normal size. What if the antidote didn't work? What if it was the wrong plant?

"Get!" he yelled.

She scrambled up the steps and threw herself down on the deck, feeling helpless. It was not an emotion she was used to feeling, and she took it hard. Every second crept by. As the sun slipped lower in the west she stood and paced, listening carefully for sounds from inside the cabin. But there was nothing.

When she could stand it no longer Rachel crept back down the steps and softly approached his berth. Flynn was sleeping. His arm was thrown back over his head, covering half his face, his bare chest rising and sinking with slow, deep breaths.

Pressing a hand to her throbbing temple, she watched him sleep. The reverend had said nothing about the victim sleeping. Hadn't the potion worked at all?

For a long time Rachel merely sat and stared at him, praying that he would be well again. When she finally stood up she was stiff, and weariness was weighing her down. She walked to the companionway and looked out at the sky. It was getting dark. Where was Pete? she wondered for the hundredth time.

A moan came from behind her. Swinging around, she rushed back to the berth. Flynn thrashed about wildly, uncaring that the nylon rope cut into his wrist. Perspiration beaded his twitching body. It was beginning.

Disregarding his orders, Rachel wet towels and bathed Flynn's face and chest continually with cold water. His free arm caught her in the face twice as she ran the cool towel over his body again and again. When his bound feet caught her in the chest, knocking her down, she pulled herself up and went back to the bunk.

Sometime in the middle of the night the wild thrashing stopped, but he still rolled back and forth restlessly. Rachel was beyond thinking. She did what she could to make him comfortable, sitting on the floor beside him during the quiet times.

He had been muttering incoherently for several hours. At first she hadn't paid attention to what he was saying; then slowly the words began to sink in.

She raised her head and stared at him in astonishment. "Dow Jones average?" she whispered hoarsely. "Futures and dividends?"

The unkempt, unconventional Flynn had once been an upwardly mobile, button-down Wall Street stockbroker. If Rachel hadn't felt so much like crying she would have laughed.

"Lili," he rasped out shortly. "Lili, I can't—when you..."

Rachel bit her lip. Lili must have been the Marquesan woman he had loved. Rachel suddenly felt like a voyeur, an intruder on his private agony. She tried to shut out the words, knowing he would hate her hearing them, but it was impossible.

"I'm sorry—I'm sorry," he moaned. "I shouldn't have left you. I should have...*Damn you!*" he shouted explosively. "Why did you have to die? Why...?"

His voice faded away, and he began to roll restlessly again. Rachel wiped the tears from her face and moved to the sink to dampen the towel again. She ached for all the old pain she felt in him.

"I'm so sorry, Flynn," she whispered as she bathed his face.

He pushed her hand away roughly. "The *bitch*," he spat out viciously, his head tossing from side to side. "She thinks I don't know what she's doing. The way she looks... the way she moves. Even the way she smells. It won't work. Do you hear? It won't work."

"Shh," Rachel said, her voice soothing. "No, of course it won't work."

On and on their battle continued; then, in the small hours of the morning, the delirium stopped as abruptly as it had begun. It was finally over.

On the bunk Flynn lay still, almost lifeless. The flesh at his wrist and ankles was raw and bleeding. Rachel didn't even bother trying to untie the ropes. Moving mechanically from exhaustion, she picked up a knife and cut them. She removed his perspiration soaked shorts, then began cleaning and bandaging the scrapes.

As she tended his wrist Flynn began to shiver. Soon the tremors became violent, shaking his whole body. "Cold." The word was merely a harsh croak. "So cold."

She hadn't expected this. The reverend hadn't said anything about tremors, either. Swinging around, she pulled the sleeping bag from her bunk. Spreading it over him, she quickly tucked it around his body. It was painful to see the weakening shudders wrack him. She wanted to scream at the top of her lungs that it was wrong—this shouldn't be happening to a man like Flynn. Flynn was cocky and strong; Flynn was life itself.

Sliding down to sit on the floor beside the bunk, Rachel prayed as she hadn't prayed in years. She prayed the earnest, sobbing, incoherent prayers of a child.

Rachel came awake in the dark with a jolt, fear ripping through her when she realized she had fallen asleep. Jerking her head toward Flynn, she ran her anxious gaze over him, then caught back a sob of relief. He had kicked aside the cover and was sleeping peacefully.

She rose stiffly and leaned over him to adjust the cover. He muttered softly in his sleep, then, without warning, reached out and grabbed her by the neck, pulling her down beside him on the bunk.

"Flynn," she whispered gently, "let go." She struggled to free herself from his arms. "I've got to get up and take care of you. I can't—"

"Be still."

Rachel stopped struggling. Glancing up, she examined his face. The brusque words had sounded almost lucid, but his eyes were closed. Sighing, she relaxed. She didn't want to disturb him, and sooner or later he would release her in his sleep.

Rolling toward her, he wrapped one leg over both of hers, pulling her lower body closer beneath the cover. When she felt the hardness of his masculinity pressing against her hip, a soft choking laugh escaped her. Even when he was half-dead Flynn didn't change; he would always be very much a man.

After several minutes Rachel cautiously began to ease away from him. Instantly his hand was on her neck. "No," he whispered so softly she couldn't be sure he had really said it.

She stiffened when she felt his lips on her neck and in her hair. "Flynn—Flynn stop." She gasped loudly when his hand found her breast.

Then his lips were on hers, and her protests were lost in the warmth of his kiss. Rachel struggled with Flynn determinedly, but it couldn't match the struggle that was going on inside her. There was no doubt that she wanted him. But she wanted him when he was awake and lucid.

He couldn't know what he was doing, she told herself as she clasped his face between her hands to push it away. If she allowed this to continue, it would be like taking advantage of his irrational condition.

Pulling his head away, she drew in a deep breath. This was all wrong. He might even think that he had his lost Lili beside him. The idea made her wince in pain. Pushing at his shoulders, she inched away from him.

"Damn it, Boston," he muttered. "Come here."

Rachel stiffened, then relaxed against him, making no protest when he tilted her head to kiss her throat. It was all right. He knew who she was.

As the weariness seeped out of her, she pressed her body closer to his, the movement urgent, because she was relieved that he recognized her, because they had fought off the terror of the poison together. And because she wanted him desperately.

His unconscious mind must have sensed her compliance because a rough sound of victory came from his throat and he held her tightly against him. Within seconds she was naked beneath his body, her limbs entwined with his.

All the desperation she had felt as she nursed him, all the anguish of seeing the man she loved so near death, were in her response to his touch and his kiss. It didn't matter that neither of them was fully conscious. The energy that flowed between them was beyond consciousness. It came from a basic, instinctive level, overwhelming them both.

Her flesh was electrified. She felt his chest against her breasts, his hard thighs against her own, the throbbing heat of his desire matching her own. His urgent hands hurt her breasts, and she laughed in pure pleasure, covering his fingers with her own. She wrapped her long legs around him, needing desperately to capture him and the sensation his touch brought.

In a mindless fury they joined together at last, need and desire and love filling Rachel as she felt his hard, hot strength inside her. He began to find emotions in her that stunned her with their force; they seemed to be bound together in a way that went beyond physical pleasure. A raging fire grew inside her heart and her loins, building to the point of pain, consuming her completely.

And then, as he loved her, she felt the brilliance of tropical stars open up in her mind. And, together, they flew.

Chapter Nine

As Rachel came slowly awake she tried to absorb and hold the warm, rich texture of the contentment pulsing through her veins. She began to stretch luxuriously, then stopped abruptly when her hand met warm flesh.

Jerking her head to the side, she ran her gaze over Flynn's features. His color was good, and he was breathing normally. She relaxed and smiled. Then, like a thief waiting in hiding to attack, the memory of their lovemaking struck her forcefully.

She closed her eyes weakly as a myriad of emotions flooded her mind. Astonishment was tinged with pleasure. Fulfillment was tainted by regret.

Easing her way from under the cover, she stood for a moment beside the bunk, her expression nervous as she pushed back her disheveled hair.

What kind of mess had she gotten herself into this time? she wondered as she quickly pulled on her clothes. Last night neither of them had been quite sane. Anxiety and exhaustion had fogged her mind, allowing her to believe that making love with Flynn was right and natural. And he had been under the influence of those damned psychedelic flowers. Neither of them had been playing with a full deck.

Glancing back at the bunk, she bit her lip. Flynn would never let her live it down. He would taunt her unmercifully for the wanton way she had behaved in his arms. He would probably try to charge her extra, she thought in disgust.

She almost moaned aloud when she remembered the way she had responded to him. Flynn was barely tolerable under normal circumstances; what would he be like now that he had an edge on her? How could she, ever for a second, have thought she loved him?

Walking to the companionway, she opened the door and stared out. It was full daylight. Where on earth was Pete? If he had been on the boat last night none of it would have happened. She frowned, her eyes troubled. What if something had happened to him?

When she heard the rustle of the sleeping bag she swung around skittishly. Flynn was sitting on the edge of the bunk, stretching his arms above his head.

"God, I feel great," he said, his voice strong and filled with sickening enthusiasm. "*Fan*tastic. I can't remember ever feeling so good."

Rachel swallowed with difficulty. Here it comes, she thought as she eyed him warily. Now the torture would begin and, knowing Flynn, he would drag it out interminably, making the most of the opportunity.

Catching her gaze on him, he said, "Where's Pete?"

She held herself perfectly still, watching his expression closely. "He's not back yet."

"What do you mean, he's not back?" Frowning, he stood up. "You mean he didn't come back at all? You took care of me by yourself?"

He didn't remember. She felt relief flood her, leaving her momentarily weak. Sometime in the distant past she must have done something very good to deserve such a reward. Flynn didn't remember the night before.

In the next second, perversely, she was irritated. How could he forget? Had her touch, her body, been so unmemorable? Hadn't he felt the explosion of sensual pleasure that had rocked her the night before?

When she realized he was still waiting for an answer she muttered, "I managed." Then, mentally cursing her illogical thoughts, she said, "You really don't remember any of it?"

"I remember falling asleep—that's all. Nothing about—" He broke off when he caught sight of the severed ropes lying on the floor. Raising his gaze to study her face, he said quietly, "Was it bad?"

"It wasn't the murderous schizophrenia Scudarri predicted," she said, ignoring the bruises on her chest where he had struck her. "I'm just glad you're all right now."

"I'm better than all right," he said expansively. "My arm isn't even sore. And I'm starving to death. We missed dinner last night."

She watched him select a piece of fruit. "What about Pete? What do you think happened to him?"

"Don't worry about Pete. He's got more lives than a Shanghai alley cat. After we've had something to eat we'll go look for him."

At that moment they heard a soft thud on the deck. Seconds later Pete blocked the sunlight in the companionway with his dripping body.

"It's about time," Flynn said, biting into a mango. "Where have you been all night?"

Pete plunked a canvas-wrapped package on the counter. "I got the carburetor."

"It took you all night?" Flynn asked dryly. "They have to build it for you?"

Pete grinned. "Actually, they had to take it off an old fishing boat, but that's not what kept me so long. I ran into unexpected company. Before we talk I need to change out of these wet shorts. Turn around, Rach." He began to unfasten the shorts.

Turning obediently, Rachel said, "What do you mean, unexpected company? Did you find Cleve?"

"No, I'm sorry," he said. "It's not this island. Okay, I'm decent."

He was fastening a clean pair of shorts when she turned around again. Grabbing an orange, he flopped down on Rachel's bunk and began to peel it.

"I walked across the island in the direction of the village, just like I was supposed to—took me about four hours." He swallowed a section of the orange whole. "There's a small crest just before you get to the other side, so I sat there for a while scoping out the place. All of a sudden two identical boats came out of nowhere. They were power boats, bigger than the *Nightingale*. Brand spankin' new—expensive mothers both of them. They landed right there beside the village and—" Shaking his head, he glanced at Flynn. "It was the damnedest thing, boss. It looked like a cheap imitation of the landing at Omaha Beach. I expected to see John Wayne any minute. These men started pouring out of the boats and running toward the village. I thought I'd stumbled into an all out Polynesian war. But the men who were attacking—" he caught Flynn's eyes "—they weren't Polynesian."

"Attacking? What do you mean, attacking?" Rachel asked in confusion.

"I mean attacking—as in 'Remember the Alamo.'"

"Go ahead, Pete," Flynn said. "What happened?"

"They had handguns strapped to their waists, but they didn't use them. They looked like they were trying to shake the villagers up without really doing them any harm." He chuckled in wicked pleasure. "But it didn't work out that way. Those villagers—man, you should have seen them. They were fighting those sons of bitches with clubs and machetes and garden hoes—anything they could get their hands on. Hell, even the kids were in on it. I've never seen anything like it. There couldn't have been more than a dozen men in the whole village, but by God they're scrappy devils. By the time I got down to the beach the white men were back in their boats. They didn't leave, though. The boats just hung offshore, like they were waiting for orders, or regrouping, or something."

He paused, finishing the orange. "I was a little nervous about letting the villagers see me—in case they thought I was one of the men from the boats. That's when I ran into Tahia. She's the chief's daughter, and luckily she speaks fluent French. They use a Polynesian dialect here that I can't make head nor tail of—sounds like Swahili or something. Anyway, Tahia says she's never seen these men before and had no idea where they came from. But when we got to Elahi—that's the village—I found out her father thinks this attack may have something to do with the fishermen."

He leaned forward, his face serious as he glanced from Flynn to Rachel. "Lately, when the men have tried to fish the waters around Iaukea—"

"Iaukea?" Rachel asked, feeling her pulse quicken. "The last island?"

"The very one," Pete said. "As soon as the fishermen get near the bay on the northeast side, white men come out in boats to run them off. Apparently these Pohukainians are a hard-headed lot. They've been fishing those waters for centuries and don't like the idea of strangers telling them the island is off-limits now. So they keep going back. The old chief thinks the invasion might be some kind of warning." Pete met Flynn's eyes. "He also thinks these men might have something to do with the Pohukainians who have disappeared recently."

Flynn glanced up sharply. "Disappeared?"

"Yeah. Weird, huh? Shades of zombies and giant pods. Four of their young people, two men and two women, simply vanished in separate incidents. One pair went to spend a couple of days at a small uninhabited island just northwest of here. They never came back, and there was no trace of them on the island. The other two had gone to the north side of Pohukaina to hunt. The old chief is convinced these boatmen took all four of them. That's why they were fighting like demons. They want their people back." He shook his head. "I can't figure it out. What do you think? Maybe slave labor?"

"Beats the hell out of me," Flynn said, his voice puzzled. "Labor's dirt cheap around here. And anyone who could afford the kind of boats you were talking about could ship people in by the dozens from the Orient."

"Yeah, that's what I thought, too. Anyway, I promised Tahia and her father I would bring back what guns we have." He laughed. "There's one rusty shotgun on the whole island." He stood up and moved to a tall locker, pulling it open. "The only thing is, we have to walk back across the island. If we try to take the *Nightingale* around, those boats might try to bushwhack us."

Flynn stood up. "Then we walk." He turned to Rachel and frowned. "I don't think they'll bother you on this side of the island, but we'll leave you a handgun just in case. If you see *anyone* who looks suspicious, use it. That little silver derringer of yours wouldn't scare a sparrow."

She rose to her feet. "You won't have to leave me anything, because I'm going with you."

"Like hell you are!" Flynn bellowed.

"I think he's right this time, Rach," Pete said, his tone sympathetic. "Those men aren't through yet. There's going to be trouble."

She began tying her hair back with a paisley silk scarf. "Then one more helping hand should be appreciated." Her chin looked like Asa's as she turned to meet the two pairs of eyes. "I'm coming."

"I can tie you to the mast, Boston—and don't think I won't," Flynn said tightly.

Green sparks flared in her eyes. "You can try," she said softly. "That little silver derringer may not be macho, but it's big enough to put a hole in your leg."

They stood almost nose to nose, glaring at each other. Then Flynn swung away from her abruptly. "You are the most bullheaded woman I've ever had the misfortune to meet," he said under his breath as he grabbed two handguns and moved impatiently toward the companionway. "And that's probably one of your better qualities."

Rachel stared after him, her face flushed in anger. When she heard laughter she swung around toward Pete.

He shook his head, chuckling as he slid the strap of a rifle over his shoulder. "Your battle awaits, m'lady," he said, his eyes sparkling. "Damned if I don't think I would back you against those invaders after all."

Inhaling slowly, she smiled. "If you're teasing me, you're as big an idiot as he is," she said sweetly. "If you're serious, you've got more perspicacity than I gave you credit for." Then she turned and followed Flynn topside.

An hour later they had passed through the portion of jungle Flynn and Rachel had explored the day before and were following a trail hacked out by Pete on his trip across the island. Thick forest crowded in on them. It was already beginning to repair the damage Pete had done the day before. Golden shafts of sunlight broke through occasionally but didn't have much effect against the overpowering green. The only sounds to disturb the all-consuming silence were their muffled footsteps and an occasional falling coconut.

By the time they broke out of the forest and entered a dry savanna where nothing grew except yellow grass and small ferns, Rachel was growing tired. Although she had always been physically active, she had had almost no rest the night before, and she was beginning to feel the lack of sleep.

Flynn watched her from the corners of his eyes. He knew she was having to struggle to keep up, but she didn't say a word in complaint. Stubborn woman, he thought, unwilling to acknowledge the strange feeling of pride that came over him as he watched her. Several times he was tempted to call for a break so she could rest, but he could guess what her reaction would be to accepting any concessions. So he kept the pace steady as he followed Pete's trail.

Rachel wasn't the only one breathing heavily when they finally topped the crest that gave them their first view of the tiny village of Elahi. There wasn't an islander in sight, giving the place a strangely forsaken look.

And out in the ocean, holding offshore, were the two boats Pete had described.

"They're still there." Flynn leaned back against a slab of rock as he watched the boats.

"Yeah," Pete said, his voice distracted as he gazed not at the bay, but at a point just below them. Raising a hand, he waved vigorously.

Rachel turned to follow his gaze. A beautiful young Polynesian woman was climbing toward them. Without a word to Flynn and Rachel, Pete started sliding down the incline to meet her.

Flynn glanced at Rachel. "Like I said—we don't need to rest. We might as well go on to the village."

She laughed. "I don't suppose that could be the chief's daughter?"

He shrugged. "Could be. Maybe she's giving him Swahili lessons."

They caught up with Pete and the girl on a beach of fine black volcanic sand. As Rachel and Flynn had suspected, the girl was Tahia, the chief's daughter. Her black hair fell in waves to her hips, making a sharp contrast to her fair skin. She had a slightly aquiline nose and sweet, shy eyes.

"We were worried about you," she said in rapid French, clasping Pete's arm between both her hands, running to keep up with him as they all walked toward the village.

"I told you I would be back," he said. "And that I would bring help." He glanced down at her. "You barely said hello to Rachel and Flynn."

Rachel smiled at Tahia, but the girl didn't notice. She didn't take her eyes—very black, very adoring eyes—away from Pete. "I'm sorry," she murmured. "I have the manners of a pig."

Flynn raised a brow. "I think you may have left out some of the details about last night, Cowboy."

Rachel expected Pete to make a flip remark, but he wasn't paying any attention to Flynn. He was staring down at Tahia in the same way she was staring at him. Pulling slightly ahead, they spoke quietly in French; then Pete glanced back at Flynn and Rachel.

"Tahia says she and her father have gathered all the islanders together. They're ready for us to take command." He frowned, his dark eyes dimming. "They're putting a lot of faith in us."

"Don't sweat it," Flynn said. "Who better to lead a battle than a couple of old barroom brawlers and a Boston deb?"

Pete swallowed a spurt of laughter. "When you put it like that, how can I doubt us?"

As soon as they entered the village, the two men left Rachel and Tahia in charge of the women and younger children, while they went to organize the men. Rachel stood watching the children scrambling around on the beach like ants on a picnic blanket.

"What are they doing?" she asked in bewilderment.

"Looking for large rocks and shells," Tahia explained in her soft voice. "And those women are gathering coconuts . . . to throw."

Rachel was stunned. These people were planning to fight guns with coconuts and rocks. And they seemed to simply take it in stride. Rachel had friends in Boston and New York who panicked if someone from out of town moved into their apartment building. The same people ran in terror to their analysts if they were snubbed at a party.

Although the admission didn't come without a certain amount of pain, Rachel finally admitted she knew nothing about the real business of living. Modern life in America had been refined and polished and push-buttoned until it was nothing more than a thinly structured web of superficialities. Scented underarm deodorant and drinks with cute names weren't what life was about after all.

As she stood on the black beach Rachel felt a twinge of something she had never experienced before—inadequacy.

"You have known Pete for very long?"

The soft question brought Rachel's gaze back to Tahia. "Actually, I haven't," she said. "It seems like

I've known them both forever, but it's only been a few days.''

The Polynesian girl dropped her dark gaze to the sand. "He likes you."

"I like him, too." Rachel hid a smile. Polynesian maiden or Boston deb—all women were the same where men were concerned. "Tahia," she said gently, "Pete and I are just friends. It's not the special kind of liking."

The girl glanced up. "He says he lives on Hiva Oa. My father went there once . . . to Atuona. He says it is an enormous place, and people—women—are everywhere. Maybe there is someone in Atuona that Pete has a special liking for."

"He hasn't said." She remembered the two girls on Mana Kula. "Somehow I don't think so," she said dryly.

Tahia smiled brilliantly, then left to help the women while Rachel worked with the children.

It was growing dark when Flynn finally made his way back to Rachel. He and Pete had done what they could in the village; now all that was left was to wait. The next move would come from the sea.

As he neared the beach he spotted Rachel immediately, her blond hair separating her from the group of laughing children that pulled her along the black sand. Frowning, he realized that her hair was the only thing that set her apart. Why should she look natural with the island children? He didn't want her to fit in so beautifully.

Turning her head, she caught sight of him and waved, quickly detaching herself from the children to run toward him.

"Is it all set?" she asked breathlessly when she reached him.

"All set," he confirmed. "Whether it'll work or not is another question."

"It's got to work," she said fiercely. "It absolutely makes my blood boil to think of those men taking advantage of the islanders. All they want is to be left in peace to raise their families and live off what the land provides. It's criminal to threaten their way of life."

Flynn stared at her thoughtfully. "You might say those men in the boats represent what we call progress. They're the twentieth century. They're condominiums and resorts. They're civilization."

"Then they can have it," she said. "What kind of progress destroys?"

The condemnation didn't strike Rachel as being in the least ironic, because at some point in the afternoon she had switched sides. Civilization now felt as foreign to her as it was to the people in Elahi.

Following Flynn's orders, Rachel and Tahia moved the women and children into one of the huts to wait. Rachel didn't argue this time. She knew she would be more useful tending the wounded in the hut.

Long, tedious minutes passed before she heard the eerie sound of a conch shell being blown somewhere on the beach. The boats were coming back.

Almost immediately they heard the sound of gunfire nearby. The loud noise frightened the children, some of whom had never heard the sound. She and Tahia began to play with them to take their minds off the noise. The island children were stoics, but they were still children.

Rachel had thought the waiting period interminable, but it was nothing to what she went through now, knowing that Flynn and Pete were in the middle of the battle. Several minutes after they heard the shots the first of the islanders was brought to the hut for treatment.

Soon Rachel and the other women were kept busy tending wounds, luckily most of them minor. When she ran out of bandages she glanced around the hut for Tahia, but the girl had disappeared.

"Tahia?" she said to one of the women.

When the older woman pointed to the door Rachel groaned. Where could the Polynesian girl have gone? she wondered frantically. Pete would kill her if she let anything happen to Tahia.

Glancing out the window, she saw that the battle had moved closer. Polynesians were fighting the invaders from three different directions, confusing the men from the boat, causing them to waste ammunition with wild shots.

Between two of the huts, Rachel saw Tahia. The girl was trying to help an older man to his feet, but he kept falling to the ground weakly.

At that moment one of the men from the boats ran around the corner of the hut next to where Tahia and the old man struggled to move. The newcomer slid to a halt, then, reaching out, he grabbed Tahia and began pulling her out into the open, using her body as a shield against the islanders' weapons.

Rushing toward the door of the hut, Rachel pulled the little silver derringer from her pocket. She had never done more than shoot cans and practice targets with the gun. She didn't know if she could use it against another human being.

Running across the clearing, she dodged islanders and invaders alike and came up behind the man who held Tahia clasped to his chest. He moved cautiously toward the beach, carrying his gun in front of the struggling young woman.

From behind him, Rachel drew a deep breath, then raised the derringer.

Flynn dove behind a barricade of tree branches he and the islanders had constructed earlier in the day. As he reloaded his pistol he peered through the shrubbery. The invaders were weakening. Already several of the men had returned to the boats. The ones who were left were no match for the fiery islanders.

When he had finished reloading Flynn stood and glanced out across the small clearing. Pete stood with his back to a hut as he and two Polynesian men battled several of the invaders. Beyond them one of the men from the boat was dragging a companion back toward the beach.

Flynn's gaze passed over three people on the edge of the clearing, then swung back urgently.

Even tied back with a scarf, Rachel's blond hair stood out like a beacon. Flynn's features were rigid as he watched her move carefully closer to one of the invaders and a Polynesian girl—Tahia.

What in hell were they doing out in the open? he wondered, feeling the urge to strangle Rachel with his bare hands. Leaping the barricade, he ran toward her, uncaring that he was drawing the fire of the few remaining invaders.

Then he slid to an abrupt halt and pulled back into the shadows. He watched for a moment, then laughed in exhilaration and pride as Rachel raised the little silver derringer and calmly shot the man who held Tahia in the foot.

The little hellion, he thought, still chuckling as he watched the two women drag an old man toward the emergency hut. The beautiful, hardheaded hellion.

After Rachel and Tahia had tended the wound of the old man they had rescued, activity in the hut began to flag. Then, almost as suddenly as it had begun, the fighting was over. The two women left the hut in time to watch the boats disappear into the night.

Rachel glanced around the clearing, then began to move through the crowd of exhausted islanders, her gaze drifting from one to the other, searching for one particular face.

"Looking for someone?"

When she heard Flynn's voice she swung around and threw herself into his arms, holding him tightly in relief.

"Are you glad to see me, or are you just resting?" he asked. The words were light, but the hand on her hair was gentle.

"Is Pete all right?" she asked, pulling away from him in embarrassment.

"He's fine. Last time I saw him, he was giving Tahia hell for leaving the hut—which reminds me," he said, "what in hell did you think you were doing? You could've gotten yourself killed."

"So could you. But I don't want to think about that now. It's over, and we all survived."

For a moment he looked as though he didn't want to let her off so easily, then he shrugged. "You're right. It's over. But next time, remember who's the captain."

She moaned. "Don't even talk about 'next time.' I've had enough warfare to last a lifetime."

"We're both tired. The chief arranged a hut for us on the beach. We can go anytime you're ready."

She glanced at him warily. "A hut? You mean for me and you and Pete."

"Actually," he said, rubbing his chin, "Pete and Tahia have probably already left."

Rachel was beginning to get nervous. She didn't like the strange tone in his voice. "Left for where?"

"They decided to go back to the *Nightingale* tonight. When Pete gets the engine fixed, they'll bring the boat around to Elahi to pick us up."

"They decided to go tonight, in the dark?" she asked in disbelief.

"Pete's *real* anxious to get that carburetor put in," Flynn said. His features were serious, but his eyes sparkled with amusement. "And he might have gotten lost without Tahia. She knows a shortcut."

"I'll bet," she muttered, then glanced up at him. "So you and I will be sharing the hut . . . alone."

"Uh-huh," he said, grinning sadistically. "But don't worry." He tweaked her nose. "I trust you."

Then he walked away, leaving Rachel swearing violently under her breath.

Rachel lay on a woven mat, staring wide-eyed into the darkness, as she had for hours. Although she had dreaded Flynn's teasing when they were alone in the hut, he had arrived much later than she had, creeping in silently as though to keep from waking her.

She heard him shift slightly, wishing sleep would come so easily to her. But even though the hour was very late, she felt wide awake. Too much had happened, and there was still more to come. She thought wistfully of the hot tub in her apartment. It always relaxed her when she was keyed up.

Moving silently, she rose to her feet and left the hut. On the beach, she stared out across the water. The moon shone brightly, leaving iridescent tracks on the ocean.

She stood motionless for a long time, then slowly, as though mesmerized by the incandescent beauty, she removed her clothes and walked into the water.

The sensuous water enveloped her, caressing her, holding her up as she swam. She rolled and dove, then burst to the surface in an excess of exhilaration. She felt wonderfully, marvelously free.

Flynn stood on the beach, unable to take his eyes from Rachel. He had followed her simply to make sure she was all right. He hadn't expected to find himself seduced by a fairy-tale creature.

Her slender body shone pure silver in the moonlight; he could almost feel the texture of it beneath his fingers. He hesitated for only a moment to strip off his shorts, then stepped into the waves.

She knew he was there even before she turned her head to meet his eyes. Neither of them spoke. Words were an unnecessary encumbrance in an enchanted place on an enchanted night. For an endless time they swam together, their bodies touching briefly, then parting, then irresistibly coming together again. They played; they tantalized; they seduced.

Then, still without a word spoken between them, they turned together and swam toward shore. When Flynn felt the sand beneath his feet he lifted her in his arms and carried her to the grassy knoll that gave way to the beach, the same knoll where he had stood earlier, watching her.

He laid her gently on the soft grass, leaning on one knee beside her. Tangled strands of hair, turned deep gold by the sea, spread out around her face, giving her a pagan, unfettered look. There were no barriers—socially, mentally, or physically—between them now. There was only urgent, mutual need.

"This time I want to be able to see you," he said hoarsely. "I want to see your face when I touch you... I want to see your face when you touch me."

"You remember." The words were a husky whisper.

"I never forgot. How could I?" His eyes blazed as he ran his gaze down her pale body. "It was an explosion that should have rocked the *Nightingale* right out of the water."

"Then why—"

"Because you didn't want me to remember. You were embarrassed." He shrugged. "Sometimes even a pirate can be a gentleman."

"Not a gentleman," she said softly. "A gentle man."

He raised his eyes to hers. "We're both awake and aware and sane now. Will you regret it again tomorrow?"

Lifting her hand, she ran her fingers slowly up his arm and across his shoulder to his throat. It took only a minimum amount of pressure to bring his head down to hers.

"Never," she whispered against his lips as their slick bodies moved together again.

"When Pete and Tahia get back with the *Nightingale*, we'll go and talk to the people. I think he can get more out of them than we can. They seem to look at him as one of them." He grinned. "I don't suppose he told them he's from Kansas." He glanced down at her. "Are you getting tired, sweetheart?"

She met his eyes, then smiled and shook her head. It was early morning. Neither of them had done much sleeping. There had been too much loving, too much discovering to do. But Rachel wasn't in the least tired. A different kind of energy filled her as they walked hand in hand along the black beach.

"Everything we've heard about Iaukea so far sounds all wrong." She bit her lip. "What if Cleve's not there? It's the last island."

"It's not the last one. It's the last big one. There are hundreds of small uninhabited islands scattered around here." His fingers tightened on hers. "Listen, sweetheart, we'll find him. I promise you that. If we have to search the whole Pacific, island by island, we'll find him."

"Maybe I should get in touch with Asa," she said thoughtfully. "He has connections all over the world. I'm positive he can dig up someone to help us."

"If we need help I'll radio Atuona. I've got a few friends there who would help if I asked them to."

"Flynn...darling," she said, forcing a smile, "I'm sure you have innumerable friends, but my father knows people in authority."

"Rachel, *love*," he said through clenched teeth, "I don't care if he knows the president of France. There are times when you need people on the other side of the law."

"Well, you should know plenty of those," she muttered under her breath.

"What? I didn't quite catch that."

"I just said I'm sure you're right, darling. However—"

"However, nothing. You hired me—*darling*—to do a job, and I'll do it without yelling for Daddy."

Rachel glared at him. "You—" she began, then broke off to swallow heavily and give him a smile that didn't quite reach her eyes. "Maybe you're right," she said tightly.

He stopped walking abruptly and dropped her hand. "This is ridiculous. Just because we made love doesn't mean we have to stop being ourselves. We're acting so damn sweet, it makes me want to puke. I'm *not* a sweet person."

Rachel drew a breath of relief. "No, you're not," she said, meeting his eyes squarely. "You're an arrogant, conceited, overbearing, dictatorial bastard. If we need help *I'll* arrange for it."

"And you're a condescending, pigheaded, spoiled rotten socialite!" he yelled. "This is my show. We'll do it my way."

For a moment they stood and glared at each other. Then Rachel began to sputter in amusement. Flynn reached out and pulled her into his arms, hugging her close as he buried his face in her hair and shook with laughter.

"That's much better," he said when they had calmed down. "We found something pretty wonderful last night. We—the dictatorial bastard and the spoiled rotten socialite. Miss Butter-wouldn't-melt-in-her-mouth didn't make me want to grab her and throw her down in the sand."

She smiled ruefully. "I'm afraid Mr. Nice Guy didn't do much for me, either." She glanced beyond him, then sucked in a sharp breath. "Flynn, look."

Out across the blue water they saw the *Nightingale*, her clean, elegant lines breathtakingly beautiful as she made her way around a point toward Elahi.

By the time Flynn and Rachel reached the small bay Pete was maneuvering the boat next to the dock. "She's all shipshape and ready to sail," he said as he and Tahia walked to meet them.

Fifteen minutes later they were all in the chief's house. Flynn and Rachel sat at the back of the large room, while Pete talked to the chief and two other men through Tahia. Twice the conversation became heated as the islanders told their story.

Finally Pete stood and moved across the room to squat beside Flynn. "They're positive the men who attacked them came from Iaukea. The fishermen say the boats look like the ones that drove them away from the island," he said, speaking softly. "And here's something new—from a distance, the fishermen here have seen some kind of huge white structure near the bay on the northeast side of the island. It wasn't there a year ago." He shrugged. "What do you make of it? It doesn't sound right. I mean, who ever heard of a cult with a setup like that? It sounds more like a secret military installation."

"We can't even speculate until we get there," Flynn said. "We're going to have to avoid the patrol boats." He glanced at Pete. "They only guard the northeast side?"

"That's the most carefully guarded side. The fishermen have been run off from all around the island, but not as often. One of them is drawing us a map, showing a protected inlet they say will hide the *Nightingale*."

"Then that's it." Standing, he glanced down at Rachel. "How about it, Boston? Are you ready to tackle the next island?"

She stared into his brown eyes, drawing strength from him. "Sure," she said. "Let's go."

Several of the islanders followed them back to the boat. Tahia was one of them. The young woman stood alone as she watched them preparing to leave. With her heart in her huge eyes, she never took her gaze from Pete. Pete, on the other hand, carefully avoided looking toward the dock.

At the last minute Flynn said, "Hey, Pete, I've been thinking. If this place is as well guarded as they say it is, we may need the people on Pohukaina to help us."

"Yeah...so?"

"So I think it might be best if you stayed here, close to the chief's shortwave. That way, if we run into trouble, we can get in touch with you, and you can bring the marines to our rescue."

Pete glanced at Tahia, then back at Flynn. "I don't know, boss. Are you sure?"

"I'm positive," Flynn said firmly. "We may need their whole fishing fleet before we're through."

Pete hesitated only a moment longer, then he smiled brilliantly and jumped the rail to the dock. Tahia was in his arms almost before he landed.

As the *Nightingale* got under way Rachel waved to the couple on the beach, then moved to stand beside Flynn at the wheel. "That was a pretty nice thing you did," she said softly.

He raised one brow. "Nice? I don't know what you're talking about. I was simply covering all the bases."

She stared at him for a moment, feeling a small sadness welling up inside her. Flynn still had the walls up...and she was on the other side.

Chapter Ten

Rachel moved to the bow and studied the horizon. Iaukea rose steadily before them, but it didn't look like an island. It looked like what it was—the rugged peak of a mountain whose base lay somewhere on the ocean floor. Volcanic towers, pinnacles and spires rose from the sea and clouds like a moss-covered castle.

"Get the map for me, Rachel," Flynn called to her from the cockpit.

Welcoming the activity—any activity—she went below and retrieved the rough map they had brought from Pohukaina. Flynn secured the wheel and spread out the tapa cloth to study the drawings the fisherman had made. After a moment he stood, handing her the binoculars.

"Look for the scarred place on the side of the mountain," he said. "The inlet should be directly below that."

Moving the glasses slowly over the contours of the land, she at last found the deep white gash and pointed the place out to Flynn. Keeping a little offshore, they followed the shoreline to the west. Although Rachel kept the binoculars trained on the island every second, they had almost gone past the cove before she saw it.

The opening at first looked like a small indentation in the shoreline, but when the *Nightingale* slipped through the narrow channel they found themselves in a deep, sheltered cove, its shores completely hidden from view by the natural tree-covered breakwater.

As soon as they had dropped anchor Flynn glanced at Rachel. "You know we have to cross the mountain. Do you want to rest, or start now?"

"Now," she said without hesitation.

He nodded. "Then let's hit it."

Since it was likely they would have to spend the night on the mountain, they packed food, water and a sleeping bag, then set out. As Flynn hacked a narrow path through the dense jungle foliage their progress was slow, but higher up the mountain, where growth was limited to prickly shrubs and low ferns, they moved with relative ease. The view behind them was breathtaking. She could see now that the bay they had entered was merely part of a submerged canyon. The *Nightingale* looked like a child's toy from this distance, but Rachel rarely paused to look back. She was too busy trying to maintain her footing on the rocky ridge they were following.

White goats, balancing on narrow ledges to graze on tufts of grass that grew in seemingly unreachable crevices, were the only form of life they saw as they climbed. When the mountain path forked Flynn paused, then chose to go to the right. That led them to a tiny green valley where a herd of wild horses grazed contentedly. On three sides the high valley was guarded by pinnacles of basalt. On the fourth side a small rise gave way to the jungle.

The thick forest seemed almost airless when they entered it, but Rachel knew that they were now descending. Flynn teased her as they walked, making her laugh and forget how tired and hot and dirty she was. An hour after they had entered the jungle they stumbled onto a wide trail.

"Was it made by humans?" she asked.

He shrugged, still staring around. "I can't tell. I don't see any cut marks on the trees, but that doesn't mean anything. The jungle grows so fast that all trace would be wiped out in a few days."

"Remind me not to stand still," she said, pushing her hair off her damp forehead.

He chuckled, wrapping his arm around her waist as they followed the trail around a sharp bend. "I don't know, you might look cute all wrapped up in vines, the leaves artfully arranged to—" He broke off, and his steps slowed.

Looking ahead, Rachel saw a small clearing and let out a gasp of pleasure.

Emerald green was reflected in the clear water of a stream. Overhead, delicate orchids grew on moss-covered limbs, with vibrantly colored butterflies flitting about them. The stream had widened in this one spot, forming a tiny, but perfect, oasis. Water tumbled and splashed over stairstep boulders in a glistening waterfall that settled briefly in a shallow, rock-lined pool before the stream continued on down the mountainside to the sea.

Dropping the backpack, Flynn pulled her forward, then knelt to drink deeply of the cold, clear water. When they had had their fill they sat on the stones lining the sides of the pool to rest.

"Look," Flynn said after a while, "we can't get much farther today. We're going to run out of light. Why don't you stay here and watch the pack while I follow the trail a ways?" When she started to protest he added, "I promise, if I get a glimpse of the other side I'll come back for you."

She hesitated, unwilling to be left out of the exploration, but too tired to go much farther. Finally she nodded. "You won't be gone long?"

"I'll follow the trail for about half an hour, and if I don't see anything by then, I'll come back."

She leaned back to rest her head on the backpack. "Okay," she said reluctantly. "I'll stay, but not because I'm tired."

"No?" He raised a brow in inquiry.

"No," she said firmly. "I'm simply catering to your masculine ego."

He laughed outright. "That'll be the day." Gazing down at her reclining figure, he smiled wryly. "If you really wanted to cater to my masculinity you'd make me stay here with you." He paused and shook his head. "No, don't beg. I really have to go." Dodging the twig she threw at him, he grinned. "When I get back we'll go back across that little valley. There was an overhang there that will give us a little bit of shelter." Pulling his gaze reluctantly away from her, he glanced at the trail ahead. "Okay, Boston, sit tight. I'll be back in an hour."

She watched him walk away, then closed her eyes. Someday, when she had time, she would have to analyze just exactly how she felt about Flynn. He seemed to be able to pull so many different emotions out of her.

She thought of the overpowering love she had felt when he was ill. Was it real, or was it merely the result of the heightened emotions of that night? There were times when she resented the way she was coming to need him and tried to pull back. Then, other times, when she felt him shutting her out, she wanted to cling to him; she wanted to shake him and say, "Look at me!"

Frowning, she moved restlessly. This wasn't right. She was with him almost constantly, and when she wasn't with him, she was thinking about him. She had to regain her objectivity. She had decided it wasn't likely that Cleve was on this island; the cult had wanted to get back to nature in privacy, and the elaborate operation the fishermen had described simply hadn't fit in with that notion. That meant the trip would be much longer than she had anticipated. She had to remember that Flynn was nothing more than a man she had hired to help her.

For the next fifteen minutes she called up pictures in her mind—pictures of her office and her apartment, pictures of the people she worked with and the men she dated, pictures of her childhood in Boston with Asa.

It didn't work. Flynn's face kept intruding; the strength and individuality of his features made everything else fade in comparison.

Sitting up, she pulled restlessly at the collar of her shirt. Her neck felt gritty and damp. She stared at the splashing waterfall for a few seconds, then stood. Flynn wouldn't be back for another half an hour at least. In that time she could get rid of the grit on her neck and the salt in her hair.

Stripping quickly, she stepped into the pool. The shallow water, barely reaching her thighs, felt icy to her overheated skin. Making a cup of her hands, she poured water over her shoulders until she was used to it; then she moved through the pool toward the waterfall.

It was pure heaven. She raised her face to the water, letting it slide over her body in a cooling rush. Lifting her hair, she leaned her head back and closed her eyes, the noise of the waterfall blocking out every sound.

The water splashing over and past her was exciting, exhilarating. All thoughts of Boston and New York were forgotten as she became lost in the unspoiled splendor.

She didn't know why she chose to open her eyes at that very second. There was no sound to alert her. But when she saw Flynn walking toward her through the water she smiled, as though this was what she had been waiting for from the beginning.

"I always figured water nymphs would be green," he murmured huskily as he reached out to cup her breasts in the palms of his hands.

She inhaled as a shaft of pleasure struck her loins. "Disappointed?" she whispered, smiling slightly.

"No." He stared at her breasts, sucking in a sharp breath when his thumbs brought her nipples to hard peaks. "Who wants to make love to a stalk of celery?"

She laughed throatily, running her hands over his bare thighs. He was so dark, so powerful. She loved to see his tanned hands on her flesh; she loved to feel the hardness of his flesh beneath her fingers.

Urging her slowly closer, he moved so that the tips of her breasts brushed back and forth across his chest in a sensual action that left her weak. Being so close and yet still separate was a torment. Grasping his hips, she moved her body closer, a moan catching in her throat when she felt his heat burning against her.

Lowering his head swiftly, he caught the sound with his lips, pressing her back against the smooth rock behind the waterfall. His kiss drained her of strength and reason. He touched off a blazing fire that threatened to consume her.

And then, there beneath the rushing water, he made love to her in a pagan rite that ignored the bounds of civilized rules and regulations. It was thrillingly erotic; it was joyfully innocent.

Stoking her emotions with fierce intensity, he brought her to a peak of pleasure that exploded in her mind and rocked her body. Through wave upon wave of pleasure she heard the cry of the victor in his throat and reveled in the joy she had brought this strong man.

Long moments later Flynn carried her to the bank and laid her on the grass. Closing his eyes, he sank beside her, holding her close. "Boston?" he whispered gently.

"Umm?" She was too lethargic to open her eyes.

"How do you manage to make me feel as weak as a kitten?" He lazily kissed her behind the ear. "Next time we make love under a waterfall, it's your turn to carry me out."

She laughed and rolled toward him, wrapping her arms around his waist as she felt her strength return in a streak of glorious exhilaration. "You've got a deal."

He groaned and sat up. "As much as I hate to mention it, it's getting late. We'd better head back to the valley."

She felt a moment of regret at leaving the pool behind, but she knew he was right.

They spent the night in a wide crevice that overlooked the high valley. The next morning, at first light, they hid their gear behind some rocks and set out.

After climbing down the basalt boulders, they again crossed the small valley and entered the jungle.

When they reached the waterfall Flynn's steps slowed, and she wondered if he, too, were remembering the day before.

Over an hour later, when the trail veered sharply to the right he stopped, studying the huge outcropping of rock before them. "Hold on a second," he said. "I'm going to climb up and check what's below us."

Leaving her on the trail, Flynn began to climb, finding toeholds in the cracks of the rock. On reaching the top he stopped abruptly and ducked down. Raising his head slowly above the rock, he whistled softly.

"What is it?" she asked. "What do you see?"

When he motioned for her to join him, Rachel looked warily at the bare rock, then inhaled deeply and began pulling herself up. When she reached him at last she wedged herself firmly in a crevice and raised her head slightly. Looking down, she let out a gasp of astonishment.

There below them set into the side of the mountain at the edge of a dazzlingly blue bay, was an enormous tri-level structure.

It was solid white, as big and elaborate as a Riviera hotel. The levels stair-stepped down to the ground. The top two floors contained pools that overflowed in a cascading waterfall to the next level. The last waterfall emptied into a huge swimming pool, which was surrounded by native stone, palms and flowering bushes.

It seemed too much to take in all at once. Next to the building, taking up two-thirds of the shore, Rachel could see elaborate tennis courts, gardens exploding with color, and immaculately trimmed golf greens. And beyond the bay, built on a coral reef, was a modern landing strip.

"My God," she whispered tightly. "What is this? It looks like a resort, but I've never heard of anything like this out here."

"And what's more important, neither have I," Flynn said, leaning against the rock to gaze at her. "A project of this size would have the whole of the Pacific buzzing. There's money here, Boston—money on a scale even you can't imagine. Not only did it take millions to build, it took millions to buy the silence of the people who built it."

"I knew this was the wrong place," Rachel said. "Cleve practically took a vow of poverty when he joined. He said they would live off the land and sleep in huts." She glanced again at the white mansion. "This can't be it."

"You may be right," he said as he began sliding back down the rock. "In any case, we'll know for sure pretty soon."

For the next thirty minutes they kept well hidden as they finished their climb down the side of the mountain, moving steadily toward the opposite side of the bay.

When they reached the cultivated section they walked parallel to the grounds, drawing ever closer to the white mansion. Through the trees they caught glimpses of people riding horses and playing tennis. Young, beautiful people, all of them dressed in white.

"It looks like an ad man's version of Mount Olympus," Flynn said, his voice dry.

Suddenly she reached out and gripped his arm. "Flynn, look," she whispered urgently.

"At what?" He peered through the trees in bewilderment.

"Do you see those two men? They've just passed that man in the khaki outfit. See, right there, with those two women?"

"What about them?"

"Look close. Flynn, I'll swear that's Yves Reynaud."

"Who?"

"Reynaud is the French playboy who made all the headlines a couple of years ago when he brutalized a young Parisian prostitute, who decided to press charges. Everyone was shocked when he got off with what amounted to a scolding from the authorities. And I'm almost sure the man with him is Karl Wilhelm Fraunhofer." When he glanced at her in inquiry she said, "He's a German industrialist and one of Germany's most famous philanthropists."

He whistled softly through his teeth. "I've heard of him. He gives hundreds of thousands of dollars to charity every year. He's also got a wife and seven children."

She glanced up at Flynn, feeling completely bewildered. "What are they doing here? What are they doing anywhere together? They're both wealthy, but

I've never heard that either of them had the kind of money it took to finance this place.''

"You got me," he said, shaking his head as he stared at the two men.

Moments later the group took a trail that led deeper into the jungle but was not a part of it. The vegetation around the trail consisted of carefully tended flowering bushes and ferns.

Staying parallel with the four people, Rachel and Flynn followed them. Suddenly the trail curved, and Rachel lost sight of them. When they heard the low laughter and conversation of several people, Flynn moved closer, with Rachel right behind him. He stopped abruptly, causing her to glance at him anxiously.

"What is it?" she whispered. "What do you see?"

He turned and looked down at her, rubbing his chin thoughtfully. "A lot of people . . . having a party," he murmured obscurely. "And it's my turn to recognize someone."

"Who?" she said, trying to see around him.

"Deke Masters." When she stared blankly he said, "He played professional football in the mid-seventies. By the time he retired he had made a fortune in real estate . . . and, some said, from betting on his own games."

"Let me see," she said impatiently.

"Look, Boston," he said, grabbing her hand to pull her in the opposite direction, "there's nothing here that will help us. Let's go back to the main grounds."

She eyed him suspiciously. "What don't you want me to see? Is Cleve there?"

"How would I know?" he asked in exasperation. "I've never seen your brother."

"Exactly. I'm the only one who could recognize him—so let me see what's going on."

He stared at her for a moment, then shrugged slowly and moved aside. Rachel stepped forward and peered through the heavy growth. In the clearing was a small, beautifully arranged hidden garden. At first she couldn't see anything, then suddenly she gasped and took a halting step backward.

Except for two men in khaki outfits who stood casually on either side, every person in the secret garden was naked and they were in some of the most imaginative combinations Rachel had ever seen.

"Is your brother in there?" Flynn asked, his voice innocent.

"Of course not," she said belligerently. "You were right. We need to get back to the main grounds."

He grinned. "You're sure you don't want to watch a while, just in case he shows up?"

When she glared at him, he laughed softly and took her hand as they headed back toward the main grounds. They had gone only a short distance when Flynn tugged on her hand, pulling her to a halt.

"What is it?" she whispered.

He put a finger to his lips and nodded toward the jungle to the left of them. Listening carefully, Rachel first heard the soft chink of metal, then she caught the sound of voices drifting through the trees. They moved carefully in the direction of the voices and, through the trees, saw another trail, wider than the first one.

Three riders on solid white horses had just passed the spot where Rachel and Flynn now stood. Rachel stared after them, concentrating on the middle rider, who was the only one wearing white riding gear. She frowned as a shaft of sunlight filtering through the overhanging branches caught his hair, turning it pure gold.

When he turned his head slightly Rachel felt a wave of dizziness weaken her. She took a hesitant step forward, reaching out to the retreating figure with a trembling hand.

Catching her arm, Flynn pulled her back into the trees. "Rachel?" he said, his voice worried.

Blinking rapidly, Rachel bit her lip to keep from crying out as she watched the three riders disappear around a bend in the trail. "I was wrong," she said stiffly. "This is the island after all. That was Cleve."

His eyes were confused as he stared at her. "But that's good . . . isn't it?"

She could only shake her head. It was too soon to put her feelings into words. It was too soon to face the fear that had struck her when she had seen his face. After a moment Flynn pulled her into his arms, holding her silently as though willing his strength into her body.

Inhaling deeply, she raised her gaze to meet his. "Flynn, something's wrong. Something's terribly, terribly wrong. His eyes were dead . . . and he's lost so much weight. God, he looked ten years older. What have they done to him?''

"Shh," he said, his voice soothing. "We've got to get back to the overhang so we can talk. If we don't leave now we'll be caught in the jungle after dark."

"I wanted to call out to him, to tell him I was here, but his eyes—my God, his eyes—they weren't Cleve's eyes."

"Rachel," he said, giving her a small shake. "Getting hysterical won't help your brother. We've got to go over our strategy so we can get him out of here."

She drew in a deep, rough breath. "Yes." She nodded jerkily. "Yes, let's go," she said, glancing once more at the trail before she let him lead her away.

"Are you ready to talk?"

It was growing dark as they sat under the overhang, staring out across the small peaceful valley. Flynn had patiently left her to her own thoughts until she could face the problem objectively. Glancing at him, she was grateful for the no-nonsense tone of his voice. "Ready," she said firmly.

"Good," he said. "I think we need to sort out what we saw down there. Tell me your impressions."

"I keep remembering the secret garden. Whatever that place is, it offers some pretty specialized entertainment. That wasn't just a few people finding a secluded spot to make out. It seemed staged...as though the garden were specifically for that purpose." She glanced up at him. "Beside the fountain there was a mirror-topped table. Did you see it?" When he nodded she swallowed heavily and said, "On one side there was an antique porcelain cup full of silver straws, and in the center of the table was—"

"Enough cocaine to make the entire population of New York ecstatically happy," he finished wryly.

"I was afraid that was what it was." She had to fight to keep her thoughts objective. Don't think about Cleve, she told herself. Just look at the facts.

"Another thing that struck me while we were coming back here—the people wearing white, no matter what their nationality, were all young and attractive, like Cleve."

He nodded. "Group A. But the two men you recognized were wearing normal clothes. I think they must be guests—Group B. Guests, and maybe permanent residents."

"Group A was deferential to Group B, as though they were employees."

"And that brings us to Group C," he said.

"Group C?"

"I didn't think you'd noticed. They were all wearing African safari outfits, probably so the guns wouldn't stand out too much. I think they were guards."

"The two men in the secret garden...the ones in the khaki outfits."

He nodded.

"I guess it's understandable. If all their guests are as wealthy as the three we recognized they must have to keep tight security against intruders."

Staring down at his hands, he avoided her eyes.

"What aren't you telling me?" she asked, studying her face. "Something about the guards bothers you. What is it?"

"I could be wrong."

"We've got to look at all the possibilities," she insisted.

He exhaled slowly. "Okay. I don't think the guards were there to keep people out."

"Then what—" She broke off and finally allowed the thought that had been in the back of her mind to surface. "You think they're there to keep people in," she said dully. "The people in white aren't employees—they're slaves."

"I'm sorry, Rachel," he said, pulling her closer. "But that's what it looked like to me."

She nodded slowly. "It's what's been bothering me ever since I saw the expression—or lack of expression—on Cleve's face. He's being kept here against his will." She shook her head. "It's too incredible. White slavery sounds like something out of the Victorian era."

"I'm afraid it still happens, but I've never heard of it on a scale like this."

She stared out at the twilight, and her chin firmed. "You might as well say it. Cleve's being kept in a high-dollar whorehouse. He must have gone through pure hell."

"We can't think about that now, Rachel. We've got to concentrate on getting him out."

She nodded. "What are we going to do?"

"I'm afraid you're not going to like this, but tomorrow I'm going back on my own."

"Flynn—"

"No, wait," he said, interrupting her protests. "I know it's going to be hard on you. Waiting always is, but I need to scout the whole area. I need to see what we're up against. And I can do that better alone."

Again she started to argue, but he shushed her. "You're anxious and you're scared, but you've got to forget your brother for a minute and be objective. I'm right."

Agreeing to stay behind was one of the most difficult things Rachel had ever done, but she knew he *was* right. As though he knew what the decision had cost her, Flynn held her tightly in his arms.

Later, under a canopy of stars, he made love to her with a fierceness that drove every thought from her mind. With his strength pouring through her body, Rachel began to think that anything was possible.

Chapter Eleven

From his hiding place in the deep crevice of a house-sized boulder, Flynn ran the binoculars once more over the bay area. A flashy medium-large jet rested on the reef landing strip. Beyond that, in open water, two yachts were anchored. Between the airstrip and the beach, small pleasure boats dominated the waters of the bay. In the wharf area three identical patrol boats were moored, and two more guarded the entrance of the harbor.

Lowering the glasses, he leaned back against the rock. There was no way to bring the *Nightingale* in to rescue Rachel's brother. Not unless security became lax at night, which Flynn very much doubted. The whole organization was too efficiently run.

When and if they managed to get Cleve away, they would have to escape back over the mountain. Flynn didn't much like the idea of being chased over the rugged terrain by a bunch of gun-toting fanatics, fanatics who were most likely a lot more familiar with the territory than he was, so they would have to do it without arousing suspicion.

Given the small army of men that lived below him, it seemed an impossible task. He didn't see how they could manage to get in without being seen—and then there was the problem of getting out again. The guards watched every move made by the people in the white mansion. They weren't likely to look the other way just because Flynn wanted them to.

Shaking his head, he shifted his position to begin the climb down. Then he suddenly remembered the look of desperation in Rachel's eyes when she had spotted her brother.

Slowly he raised the glasses again. There had to be a way, he told himself. No system was flawless.

Out in the open ocean an ancient cargo boat chugged its way toward the break in the coral reef. It was perhaps fifty feet long and looked as though it should have been at the bottom of the ocean long ago. Before it even drew close both patrol boats were beside it. At this range Flynn couldn't see what took place, but soon the patrol boats had backed off, allowing the cargo boat to continue into port.

Moving his head slightly to the right, he picked out the wharf area again, then smiled in satisfaction. It was on the far side of the white mansion, concealed from it by a small tree-covered point. And, most important, the jungle ran almost to the docks.

Backing up and out of the narrow crevice, Flynn left the boulder and began to make his way around the northwest side of the mountain. He moved parallel to the bay, keeping high enough to avoid the white mansion.

By the time he reached the other side, the cargo boat had docked and was being unloaded. Large wooden crates and cardboard boxes were being transferred to the dock, then loaded by others onto the electric golf carts. Several poorly dressed Polynesian men, presumably the men from the boat, worked under the close supervision of four of the khaki-uniformed guards.

At that moment, as though he were bored and needed to liven things up, one of the guards seemed to deliberately step in front of a small, wiry man carrying one of the crates. The worker grunted in surprise, then shouted a French vulgarity, raising his head as he did so.

Flynn watched the confrontation, his eyes narrowing. Suddenly a slow grin spread across his face.

It was Pete.

Rachel pushed herself away from the rock and turned around in agitation. Flynn had been gone for hours. She was hot and irritable, and she was tired of waiting. Reaching down, she pulled the pink paisley scarf from the pack and tied her hair back, then glanced out across the small valley for the thousandth time.

She should have gone with him, she told herself in frustration. She belonged down there, searching for Cleve, not stuck in a hole in the rock. She shouldn't have let Flynn talk her into staying behind.

Sighing, she picked up the canteen and took a drink of the tepid water. She knew she wasn't being fair. The sight of Cleve the day before had sent her into a tailspin; she couldn't guarantee that it wouldn't happen again. She was too emotionally involved to be of much help to Flynn.

On the other side of the valley one of the wild horses shied at something red that lay in the tall grass. Rachel stood still, staring at the object. Was it moving, or merely fluttering in the light breeze? she wondered. Moving closer to the edge of the rocks, she strained her eyes for several minutes, trying to make out what it was. It could have been a shirt or a scarf, but without the binoculars she couldn't be sure.

Swinging around, she pushed the pack out of sight behind some rocks, then began to climb down the rock face. This time, when she crossed the valley, she felt vulnerable and very much alone. She hadn't realized how much confidence she had drawn from Flynn.

The grazing horses seemed to accept her presence, but stayed well away from her. When she reached what she thought was the right area she began searching through the tall grass. It had to be here somewhere, she thought, biting her lip. Even though she moved carefully, she almost stepped on the bush before she saw it. Bright crimson flowers covered it, making it appear almost solid red.

Feeling slightly foolish, she bent to pick one of the flowers, then stood and wiped her forehead as she glanced around. The jungle lay only yards away from her. It would be cooler there. Where was the stream they had found the day before? she wondered, her eyes brightening. The spring that fed it shouldn't be more than a few yards into the jungle. She would stay just long enough to cool off, she decided, then go back to the blasted cubbyhole.

Making her decision instantly, she finished traversing the valley and moved into the thick vegetation. As she carefully skirted an area thick with vine entangled bushes, she laughed softly. Flynn would kill her if she ran into a *faufau* bush.

Through the heavy silence she heard the sound of water splashing over rocks and knew she was getting close. Even the sound was cooling. Breaking through the bush, she came upon the stream suddenly. The narrow clearing wasn't as spectacular as the pool and waterfall where they had made love, but the cool, green beauty of it immediately began soothing her frazzled nerves.

Pulling the scarf from her hair, Rachel bent down to dip it in the water and wipe her face. The sparkling clear water was cold and felt sinfully luxurious on her hot flesh. She knelt on a large flat rock and dipped her cupped hands into the stream to drink.

When she had taken her fill she stared for a moment at her reflection in the water. It was a strange experience. She couldn't remember the last time she had looked into a mirror. Yes, she thought with a smile, it was on Mana Kula. She remembered how carefully she had prepared herself to meet "real" people. That day seemed a lifetime ago.

Then suddenly, as she stared into the water, another reflection appeared above hers. Catching her breath she began to swing around. Before she could complete the movement she felt a blinding pain in her head; then there was only darkness.

Flynn shifted his weight and kept his eyes on Pete. The men had been unloading for over an hour, but it looked as though they were finally heaving the last of the cargo onto the golf carts that would carry it to the mansion.

When someone tossed a mesh bag to the boat's captain he called to the others and headed for a nearby coconut palm. The others gathered around to get their share of the fruit and sandwiches the captain was passing out. Pete laughingly pushed in front of the other men, causing a good-natured argument to erupt.

Flynn, watching from his hiding place, grinned. His friend seemed to be nothing more than one of the workers; no one other than Flynn would know the younger man was carefully observing everything around him. When Pete glanced in his direction, Flynn stepped away from the tree just far enough for Pete to register the movement, then stepped back again, watching the remaining guard from the corner of his eye.

Pete grew still for a moment, but that was the only indication that he had seen Flynn. Turning back to the other men, he joined in their raucous laughter. It was only when they had finished eating and began passing a bottle around that Pete finally stood and began walking casually toward his friend.

He had gone several yards when the guard stopped him. Flynn could hear Pete tell the man in very bad French that he was simply answering the call of nature, but the guard shook his head vigorously, pointing to some bushes in the opposite direction as he spoke.

While Pete stood arguing, Flynn slid back into the forest. He moved quickly but carefully through the thick undergrowth, skirting the area next to the beach. When he arrived, out of breath, at the other side, he expected to find Pete waiting for him, but his friend still stood in the same place, arguing with the guard. Finally a shout from the captain of the cargo boat brought a resentful shrug from Pete, and he turned toward the bushes.

As Pete approached, Flynn said in a low voice, "I'm right behind the flowering bush . . . and if you pee on me, you're one dead sailor."

Pete chuckled, glancing over his shoulder to make sure the guard wasn't watching. "I do believe the quality of people you meet while taking a leak is deteriorating," he said, his voice regretful.

"I thought I told you to stay on Pohukaina."

"That's what you said, all right." He turned back toward Flynn. "Man, what have you gotten us into this time? Have you ever seen a setup like this?"

"No, thank God," Flynn said. "How in hell did you get here?"

"Tahia made me come," Pete said. "Haii, the captain of that junker in the harbor, is her mother's second cousin twice removed, or something like that. He put in at Pohukaina to see the family, and when she saw how interested I was in what the old man had to say she kicked me out of the hut." He grinned. "She looks sweet on the outside, but I think I hooked me a tiger this time. She said I had to go help my friends."

"I'll congratulate you later," Flynn said. "Right now, tell me what her uncle said that was so interesting."

"He said the boat that usually brings supplies here—a boat owned by the same man who owns the island—broke down on its way from Tahiti. The captain got in touch with Haii and promised him a huge bonus if he could get the supplies here by today. It's a one-time deal only," Pete said, keeping his voice low, "and the weird part is they won't let any of us move away from the docks. What have they got hidden on the other side of that point?"

"I'll tell you about it later." Flynn grinned. "I never thought I would be glad to see your ugly face. Remind me to kiss Tahia next time I see her." He paused, his face growing serious. "Rachel's brother is here. And, if she's right, not because he wants to be. Do you think you can get away without attracting attention?''

''I checked that out before we got here. The guy who called Haii warned him that the patrol boats would check to make sure as many men left as came in. The only thing is, they didn't count Haii's cousin, who was hiding under some equipment. As soon as I get a chance, probably just before the boat leaves, the cousin will take my place.''

Flynn nodded. ''Good. Now listen, when you go back out on the beach, check the other side of the bay on the mountainside. There's a bare place—solid gray rock. When you get away, head for the cliff just above that. I'll get Rachel, and we'll meet you there to make our plans.''

''Gotcha.'' He turned around and walked back toward the other men.

Shaking his head at the cocky set of his friend's shoulders, Flynn moved back into the jungle. Climbing high, he crossed to the other side of the bay, staying at the same height until he came across the stream that would lead him back to the small valley—and Rachel.

He climbed quickly, almost running as he made his way up the mountain. She was probably going crazy up there all alone, he thought. Even though he would more than likely be treated to a fit of temper, he was anxious to get back to her. He wanted to tell her all he had seen, and about Pete and the boats and the guards.

Hell, he swore silently. Why not admit it? He was anxious to get back simply because he wanted to see her, because he wanted to feel her in his arms again.

When he passed the waterfall he knew he was getting closer and quickened his steps. It was only a short distance now to the high valley and the overhang where they were camped.

As he rounded a bend his steps faltered slightly when a bit of unexpected color caught his eyes. Something was caught in the ferns at the edge of the pool. Staring at it, he took a halting step forward, then bent over the pool, freeing the object from the ferns. It was a paisley silk scarf.

Glancing around frantically, he took in the trampled ferns on the edge of the stream. Flynn's heart began pounding crazily in his chest. Swinging around, he tore through the jungle, automatically dodging trees and bushes as he ran. He burst upon the valley, scattering the horses as he made for the rock ledge.

Even before he reached the overhang Flynn knew he would find it deserted. He searched the small area and found the pack hidden behind some rocks. Clutching the scarf tightly in his fingers, he moved to the edge of the rock and stared out across the valley.

"RAA-CHEL!"

A flock of white doves exploded into the air, filling the sky. The wild horses stopped grazing, their ears pricking up instantly. The eerie cry seemed to go on forever. It was a sound they recognized. It was the sound of an animal in pain.

Chapter Twelve

Rachel moved her head slightly, then moaned when a sharp, red flash of pain struck behind her closed eyes. Holding her head perfectly still, she raised her eyelids. Slowly she took in the part of the room she could see without moving.

It seemed a pleasant sort of room. Nothing there to frighten her, she thought as she examined the ice blue walls and modern furniture. But why were there no windows? Rolling carefully, she stared at the opposite side of the room. No windows there, either.

This was definitely not her bedroom, she thought, the observation causing her no real alarm. Her bedroom had French windows from floor to ceiling, so she could catch as much sun as possible in New York.

Since childhood, Rachel had hated being in enclosed places. It always brought a claustrophobic tightness to her chest.

"I need to get up," she mumbled unsteadily. "Got to find out what's going on. Flynn will tell me...Flynn..."

She drew in a sharp breath and, as acutely as the pain had come before, the memory of Flynn and the islands struck her now.

Forgetting her head, she sat up abruptly, then grasped the side of the bed when the room began to swim around her. Dropping her head to her knees, she took deep, slow breaths until the world began to right itself. Then, once again, she examined the bedroom.

The wall behind the bed wasn't ice blue. It wasn't painted at all. Rising, she moved to touch it. It was gray and smooth and looked man-made, but she knew what it was—it was part of the mountain. She was inside the white mansion.

Moving quickly to the door, she tried the knob, twisting it back and forth in frustration. It was locked. Her fists clenched tightly at her sides as she fought the urge to beat on the door. Losing control would get her nowhere.

Turning slowly, Rachel returned to the bed and sat down. She had to think. She had to get past the throbbing in her head and plan how she intended to handle the situation. If only her mind were clearer, she thought, frowning. Everything was so hazy. She could remember stooping to dip water from the stream; then a face had appeared in the water. She had barely had time to recognize the khaki uniform before she had been struck from behind.

The memory brought a shiver of apprehension. She had to get her wits together before someone came to question her. She needed to decide what she would tell them.

Frowning, she went back over the night in Mana Kula. As far as she knew Jean-Paul hadn't mentioned her presence on the island. She would just have to hope that no one on Iaukea knew that she had been with Flynn and Pete that night. She would have to bluff.

You can do it, she told herself firmly. How many times had she successfully bluffed in business? If she stayed calm she could handle it. She had to, not only for herself, but for Cleve and for Flynn.

For long moments she sat, head in hands, going through the possible explanations. Whoever was in control of the elaborate setup she had fallen into was not stupid. Rachel had no room for error. If she failed to convince her captors that her presence on Iaukea was innocent, she would be no use to herself or her brother.

Jerking her head sharply to the right, she listened to the sound of a key in the lock. Rising to her feet, she watched as the door opened wide and a man stepped into the room.

Rachel's first impression was that her visitor was incredibly tall, but when she forced herself to look at him objectively she realized that he was no more than average height. However, there was something about him, something about the way he carried himself, that gave the illusion of height.

The minute she met his steady gaze she knew who he was. His eyes appeared to have no color at all. Like unflavored gelatin, they merely reflected the color of his gray hair. Looking at them made her strangely uncomfortable. It was as though she could see right into his mind.

Cleve had described him too well, she thought as perspiration dampened the palms of her hands. This was Bruce.

"Welcome to my island," he said politely. His voice was strong and musical. It pulled at her as much as his eyes repelled.

She sat down slowly, keeping her gaze on him. "Well, it's about time someone came to check on me. What in hell is going on here? Is—is this your home?"

Surely a little desperation, a little fear, would sound normal under the circumstances, she thought, moistening her lips nervously.

When he didn't answer immediately, her lips curved in a hesitant smile. "I wanted to see people—anyone human as a matter of fact—since I thought the island was deserted. But I didn't count on getting my head bashed in. If that's an old Polynesian custom I think I prefer New York subway etiquette—at least you know what to expect."

He threw back his head and laughed. Staring at him, Rachel said again, "Who are you? Do you live here?"

Moving with supreme confidence, he sat on the bed beside her. "If you will be patient and give me some information I will answer all your questions, my dear." He trained his clear, liquid eyes on her face. "May I have your name?"

"Why not?" she said, shrugging. "I'm not using it at the moment. It's..." She swallowed heavily. "Sabrina. Sabrina Pierce."

Rachel had used the first name that popped into her mind. She had completely forgotten that she would need a new name. The error made her nervous. What else had she forgotten?

"Well, Sabrina, tell me how you came to be on my island." He glanced down at his hand where it rested lightly on his thigh. The nails were shiny and too long. Raising his gaze abruptly, he met her eyes squarely. "Unless you are a mermaid, I think you must have come by boat. Where is that boat now?"

His very movements—glancing at his hand, then quickly back to her face; the way his fingers lightly stroked the fabric of his linen slacks—seemed calculated to unnerve her.

"I have no idea," she said firmly, lifting her chin slightly in an effort to meet the unspoken challenge this man posed. "If there is any justice at all it will be rotting at the bottom of the sea. The idiots left me behind," she said, her voice heavy with disgust. "They were probably stoned out of their minds, as usual. I'll be lucky if anyone remembers me before they reach Hawaii."

"Someone left you?" He raised a thick gray brow. "Who would leave such a lovely woman behind?"

Rachel smiled in acknowledgment of the compliment. "It was Pookie—Pookie Davenport of the Charleston Davenports." She stood abruptly. "I should have known better than to listen to her. She always gets me in trouble. Stealing that car on graduation night was her idea...and the date she fixed up for me with that awful Italian count!" She swung around to face him, her expression belligerent. "He was sixty if he was a day...and fat! I can't abide fat men. They always have sweaty palms."

"It was Pookie's boat?"

"Yacht," she corrected absentmindedly as she resumed her place on the bed. "Yes, it's hers...or, at least, it's her parents'. She called last month and said I simply had to join her in Hawaii. She was having the party to end all parties on the yacht, and they would simply *die* if I didn't join them." She glanced at him. "Well, that sounds innocent enough, doesn't it? Innocent hell. We didn't have one calm day at sea, and Pookie ran out of Dramamine, and I was as sick as a dog the whole time. On top of that she had collected a bunch of absolute freaks on board. You wouldn't believe the things they did...and expected me to do."

"I'm sorry you had a bad time," he said, gazing at her sympathetically. "However, that still doesn't explain how you came to this particular island."

"I don't even know where this particular island is," she complained, letting a little bit of a whine enter her voice. "I only know that it finally calmed down and things began to pick up a little. Chad—he was the only one on board who had any class at all—'' she frowned ''—or, at least, I thought so at the time. Anyway, Chad got tired of Pookie and started paying attention to me.''

She laughed in satisfaction. ''You should have seen her face. I'm surprised she didn't throw me overboard.'' She stopped suddenly and looked at the man beside her, her eyes wide. ''Come to think of it, that's pretty much what she did, isn't it? Why that little bitch! Just wait until I get my hands on her. I'll—''

''Sabrina,'' he said, gently interrupting her tirade. ''What happened when you arrived at this island?''

''What?'' She stared at him, a scowl marring her features. ''Oh, yes. The island. Yesterday—at least, I think it was yesterday—we anchored somewhere on the other side. Chad and I took a bottle of champagne and decided to come ashore—a kind of picnic.''

When he raised a questioning brow she lifted her chin and glanced away. ''There was no privacy on the yacht, and I draw the line at making it in front of all those freaks.''

''I admire your principles,'' he said softly. Rachel sensed rather than heard the mockery in his voice. ''And after you came ashore, what happened then?''

''We drank the champagne, then after, um, later, I must have fallen asleep.'' She pushed a hand through her tangled hair. ''When I woke up it was late, and Chad was gone. So was the yacht.'' She closed her eyes. ''I have never been so terrified in my life.''

Glancing at him, she grinned. "It's hell thinking you're stuck in the jungle without even Tarzan around to rescue you. I thought if I could get to a high place I could see if anyone lived on the island. I felt like a mountain climber. Just look at my legs," she said, running her hand over a scratch on her thigh. "I'm scarred for life."

"It would take more than a scratch to spoil those legs, my dear."

"They are nice, aren't they?" she said, staring in admiration at her own legs. Then she glanced up. "I've answered your questions. Now will you answer mine?"

"Of course," he said amiably. "We made a bargain. What would you like to know?"

"Who are you? Is this your house? Why was the door locked? Who tried to put a dent in my head?"

"Wait," he said, laughing. "One at a time. My name is Bruce. I live here, so I guess that makes this my home. It is also my place of business...a sort of resort. I'm sorry about the locked door and the bump on your head. But you see, we have many wealthy guests here. My men have orders to take every precaution to guard their privacy...not to mention their possessions."

"A resort?" she said, brightening at once. "Then you'll have telephones. I can arrange for transportation back to Hawaii."

"Certainly," he assured her. "If that's what you want. However, wouldn't it be easier to simply wait for your friends to return for you?"

She gave an unladylike snort of disgust. "It could be weeks before they discover I'm missing. And when they do, I'll bet you anything they don't even remember where they left me. The captain was either an idiot or he was on something. No, I think I'd better make my own arrangements...oh," she added, as though she had just thought of something, "I'd better call the States, too, and let my parents know I'm safe. I wouldn't put it past Pookie to call and tell them I had washed overboard in the middle of the Pacific. She would let me rot on some godforsaken island just to save her own hide."

He stared at her for a moment. "And they would have no way of knowing you were on my island all the time?"

She laughed. "Yes, that's why I need to get in touch with them before Pookie does."

He stood. "You can take care of all of that in just a short while. First, we must feed you. I can't have my guests going hungry."

"Food?" She stood, too. "That sounds wonderful."

Opening the door, he motioned to someone in the hall. "You will enjoy this," he said, watching as a young woman wearing a white uniform brought in an elegant tray of food and set it on the table beside the bed.

"Oh, by the way," he said, taking a few steps toward her, "tonight we are having a costume party. Since you will be my guest at least for tonight, why don't you join us?"

"What fun!" she exclaimed. "The last time I went to a costume party was in Rio two—no, three years ago."

"That's settled, then," he said in satisfaction. "I will have someone bring you a costume—something that suits those long legs."

Rachel smiled, waiting for him to leave, but he stood in the middle of the room, staring at her.

"Before I leave, I'd like you to taste the drink we've provided," he said softly, keeping his liquid gaze on her face. "It's my own recipe. You won't find anything like it anywhere else in the world."

"Your own recipe?" She looked at the glass, feeling her nerves stretch to the breaking point. "Somehow you don't look like a bartender."

Rachel was stalling for time, but even before Bruce began to move toward her, she knew it wouldn't work.

Picking up the tall crystal glass, she examined it. "I'm glad it doesn't have a piece of pineapple in it—or a paper umbrella," she said, laughing unsteadily. Raising the glass to her lips, she pretended to take a sip. "Umm, it's lovely." She raised the drink to him in a toast. "My compliments to the inventor."

"No, no, you must drink it all," he said, smiling pleasantly. "I insist. It will relax you and make you happy. I want all my guests to be happy."

She shrugged. "Whatever you say."

Lifting the glass, she fought to keep her hand from shaking as she turned it up and drained it. Then she glanced around the room. "I feel like I should shatter the glass in a fireplace, but there isn't one."

"An oversight on my part," he said apologetically as he walked toward the door. "You'll find a robe in the bathroom if you want to bathe after you eat. And someone will bring your costume in plenty of time for the party."

She sat down on the bed and stared at the tray until she heard the key turn in the lock. Then she jumped up and ran to the bathroom. Moments later, she emerged, a wet washcloth pressed to her face.

It hadn't taken much effort on her part to force the drink from her stomach. The very thought of the man who had just left the room made her ill.

She shook violently as she sat on the bed again. There was something evil about this place, and about the man who ran it, she thought, running an unsteady hand over her damp brow. The drink he had insisted she swallow had been drugged. There had been a strange undertaste that still clung bitterly to the inside of her mouth.

It would make her happy, Bruce had said. She would have to remember that. He was evil, but he was also intelligent. He wouldn't accept her automatically. She would be watched every second she was not in this room.

Leaning her head against the cold stone wall, Rachel closed her eyes. She felt drained of energy and emotion. There seemed very little she could do to help herself, and even less she could do to help Cleve. It was all up to Flynn now.

Chapter Thirteen

Flynn climbed around a large piece of jutting rock, then slid down the remaining five feet to the small rock shelf where Pete lay propped up on his elbows.

The younger man turned his head lazily when he heard Flynn's noisy approach. "That's some kind of beach cottage they've got down there," he said. "No wonder they wouldn't let us get a look at it."

"Did you have any trouble getting away?"

Pete chuckled, his black eyes sparkling. "What do you think? No freaks wearing designer safari suits can outwit me. You can call me Papillon from now on." He stood up. "The cargo boat is safely out in open ocean by now. Now tell me what the hell—" He broke off, animation draining from his features as he examined Flynn's face. "What's wrong? Where's Rachel?"

"She's gone," Flynn said, biting off the words shortly. "I think she's down there." He nodded briskly toward the bay, and his fingers tightened around the pink scarf. "I think someone found her and took her against her will to the white mansion."

Flynn felt a tightness in his head and an ache in his chest. A suffocating, mortal ache—the kind he had felt when Lili died. Only this time there was also anger. He would kill anyone who touched Rachel, kill them with his bare hands, if necessary.

Pete's face was grim as he spat out an obscenity. He inhaled slowly. "Okay, what's the plan? How are we going to get her out?"

"There isn't one . . . yet. We'll have to decide what to do when we find out where they're keeping her."

Pete nodded. "A couple of the guards were talking about a party they're having tonight—that's why they needed the supplies so urgently. The confusion of the preparations might give us a chance to find out what's going on." He paused. "You all right, boss?"

Flynn stooped to remove a piece of fern from his shoe. "Of course I'm all right," he said roughly. "We'd better get moving. I'll explain the setup on the way. By the time we get down there it'll be almost dark."

Without waiting for Pete's reply Flynn began to climb down the bare rocks toward the concealing jungle. As he had predicted, the sun had already faded into the trees when they arrived at the edge of the grounds. After crossing the bridle path they skirted the softly lit secret garden and moved closer to the white mansion.

Through the foliage they could see activity on the grounds. Pete whistled softly through his teeth. "Take a look at those costumes. This is my kind of party."

Moving the leaves of a tall fern, Flynn studied a couple not twenty feet away from them. The woman was dressed as Marie Antoinette, her white headdress outrageously high. The white wide-hipped dress was trimmed with elaborate gold embroidery. When she turned slightly toward them, they could see that the bodice of the dress was sheer white lace, exposing gold-tipped breasts. The man beside her wore a skimpy white loincloth and gold sandals.

"Everyone's wearing white and gold," Pete whispered, nodding toward a young woman who wore a sheer white and gold sari. "Is it some kind of trademark?"

"Those will be the . . . permanent residents," Flynn said. "Having them wear the same color is a good way for the guards to keep an eye on them."

"Apparently not everyone resents being here," Pete said dryly. "Check out the two fairies...they look like they're having a great time."

Several yards away a buccaneer in tight white pants, white knee boots and a flowing, gold shirt stood arm in arm with a slim young man wearing a white Roman toga cinched with a golden rope. The buccaneer stared for a moment toward the path to the secret garden, then whispered something to the other man. The

Roman laughed and nodded. Glancing around furtively, the pirate began to move nonchalantly toward the path.

"Do you suppose they're arranging a rendezvous?" Flynn asked thoughtfully.

Pete glanced at him. "What do you care?"

Flynn kept his eyes on the pirate, nodding in satisfaction when the man ducked into the path. "Maybe I'm just jealous."

"In that case, don't stand so close to me," Pete muttered. "Now where are you going?"

Stepping back, Flynn turned and ran deeper into the jungle with Pete at his heels, still muttering under his breath. They arrived at the path to the secret garden a few seconds before the buccaneer. When the man passed Flynn jumped out behind him, slamming his clasped fists into the back of his neck. Before the pirate hit the ground Flynn caught him under the arms and silently pulled him into the jungle.

Pete gave Flynn a thumbs-up gesture and waited beside the path. As Flynn began to remove the pirate's clothes he heard a loud grunt, then the soft slither of a body being dragged. The slender Roman was beginning to rouse when Pete slung him down beside the partially disrobed buccaneer. Picking up a stout stick, Pete calmly hit him again.

"You're losing your touch," Flynn said, grinning as he slid the gold shirt over his head and tucked it into the tight white pants he now wore.

"No way." Pete pulled the toga off the unconscious man. "He's just a hardheaded son of a bitch."

He held the toga up against his body. "Wise choice. It'll show off my legs. How are you doing with the pirate gear?"

"The boots are half a size too small, but the rest is all right." Flynn grimaced as he pulled on the white boots. "Where did his hat go?"

Pete glanced up from lacing the gold straps of the sandals up his calves. "Right behind you, by that tree. I hope you know what we're doing," he said wryly, "because I don't."

Flynn adjusted the gold eye patch, then shoved the wide hat on his head. "We're going to wing it. Wherever she is, we'll have a better chance of getting to her if we're unobtrusive," he said grimly. "Are you ready?"

Pete stood up and grinned as he set a crown of gold leaves on his head. "It's party time."

"Not quite. I don't want these guys waking up and spoiling things. Help me move this one to that tree."

Using part of the gold rope from Pete's costume they secured the first man's hands behind the tree, then turned to the other one.

"Separate trees?" Pete asked, shaking his head as they dragged the slender man to a tree four feet away from the one where the first man was sitting. "That's cruel, man. They probably want to be together."

"Give me the belt from your shorts and stop being such a softie."

When they were sure both men were secure they turned again toward the white mansion. Pete frowned, glancing at Flynn. "You really think we can get away with this? What if they know all the permanent residents by sight?''

"If the guards knew every one of the residents there would be no need for the identifying colors. They'll be more likely to know all the guests. All anyone will see is two men wearing gold and white—just like everyone else who works in the place." Peering through the trees, he stared grimly at the white mansion. "Okay, let's go."

Stepping out of the jungle, they unobtrusively joined a group of residents who were making their way toward the mansion. When they reached the pool area a middle-aged, buxom woman rose unsteadily from a padded lounge chair. Her red blouse and short black leather skirt resembled a streetwalker's outfit. The group of residents slowed and stopped as she looked them over.

"You ever read *The Time Machine*?" Pete whispered, leaning toward Flynn. "I feel like one of the Eloi being ushered into the Morlocks' subterranean dining room."

"I believe we're already acquainted," the woman said as her gaze traveled over a tall young man whose white suede loincloth and gold feathers bore little resemblance to the American Indian he was evidently portraying. "Yes, I'm sure we are." She glanced over the group, then stopped and returned her gaze to Pete.

"You," she said in triumph. "A Roman senator is just what I'm in the mood for."

Moving to stand beside him, she pulled his head toward her and whispered something in his ear. Pete's eyes grew round as he stared down at her, and for a moment his breathing seemed to be impaired. Glancing at Flynn, he shrugged and walked away with the woman.

Flynn stared after Pete for a moment, knowing he could trust his friend to be there when he needed him, even if Pete had to hog-tie the woman. When the group began to move again, Flynn followed.

Skirting the pool, they entered the mansion through a wide doorway that was part of a wall of glass. As the others began to spread out through the room, Flynn moved into the shadows to observe.

Costumed people of all sizes and ages moved about the enormous lounge. The white and gold clothing worn by the permanent residents seemed to blend into the furnishings, while the garish costumes of the guests stood out vividly. Clowns, matadors and sheiks mingled with white and gold clad water nymphs and belly dancers. Flynn raised one heavy brow when he saw one young woman wearing nothing more than white and gold paint.

The lounge, carved deep into the side of the mountain, was much larger than it looked from the outside. At the back of the room, behind a band of calypso musicians, were a number of doors, and white curving stairs led to the next level.

Flynn's face grew grim as he ran his gaze about the room. It would take hours to explore the entire place. But even if it took days, he would find Rachel somehow.

Skirting the crowd, he quickly climbed the stairs to the second level. The music and voices of the revelers faded slightly as Flynn entered a deserted hallway, staring at the numbered doors on either side. Cautiously he began trying them.

The twelve rooms on the first stretch of corridor were all locked. As he glanced around for something to pick the lock, Flynn stopped abruptly and watched in taut silence as a man in a khaki uniform walked toward him.

"You! Hey, you," the man called as Flynn began to turn away from him.

Flynn glanced over his shoulder. "Yeah!" he said irritably, as though the man were merely an annoyance.

"What are you doing up here?"

"Room one-fifteen sent for me."

"One-fifteen?" the man said thoughtfully.

He rested his hand on the gun strapped to his waist in what Flynn hoped was a casual movement. Hanging from the front of his belt was a large key. As though it were labeled, Flynn knew this was the master key to the guest's rooms.

"Ramsey?" The guard frowned in distaste. "Are you sure?"

Flynn shrugged. "That's what they told me."

The guard whistled in surprise. "I never would have thought it. He looks so masculine. It just goes to show you never can tell. And he asked me to have a drink with him after I get off duty."

"I wouldn't do it," Flynn advised confidentially. "Not unless..." He let the word fade away in inquiry as his gaze skimmed the guard suggestively. Sidling closer, he smiled and ran his eyes over the man's slender body. "You could always come along and check it out."

The man straightened his shoulders, throwing out his chest in an attempt to look more manly. "Of course not," he said belligerently and began to move away. Flynn stumbled deliberately into his path, forcing the other man to bump against him. In his rush to get away, the guard didn't see the flash of metal as a transfer took place.

"You get on with your work and stop loitering in the hall," he called over his shoulder.

Flynn nodded, hiding a grin as he glanced down at the key in his hand. After waiting a few seconds to let the guard leave the area, Flynn began opening doors.

An hour later he was fighting frustration. He had checked both upper levels and had found nothing. Everyone was below at the party. The doors at the back of the lounge would be his next target.

Rachel leaned closer to the man beside her, pretending to listen as her gaze drifted around the lounge. She smiled and laughed indiscriminately. Bruce had said the drink would make her happy, so happy she would be. So far, no one had seemed suspicious.

She had dreaded facing anyone, not knowing exactly how she would act if she had really taken the drug. But when the girl who brought her costume noticed nothing strange, Rachel began to feel she could pull it off.

She felt exposed and ridiculous in the costume Bruce had chosen for her, but she had made no objection. She was happy. She was so damned happy her face hurt.

As soon as she had entered the lounge the short, obese man beside her had attached himself to her firmly. Since his sole interests seemed to be eating and complaining about his wife, Rachel stayed with him, hoping his presence would keep the other guests away.

Then, as she glanced around the lounge, her heart jerked in her chest. Cleve stood not ten feet away from her. She ran her gaze anxiously over his face. He looked even worse than he had the last time she had seen him. There was something old and tired about his eyes, a look that made her want to strangle the man who had brought him here.

As though sensing the intensity of her gaze, he turned his head, and their eyes met. He blinked slowly in confusion, then swayed slightly, taking a hesitant step toward her.

Rachel shook her head in a short, almost undetectable movement. For a long, tense moment he didn't seem to understand her action and merely stood looking at her in confusion. He shook his head as though to clear it, then, his eyes opening wide, he glanced around the room in fear. When he turned his gaze back to her, Rachel cut her eyes toward a plush satin-lined alcove to her left, then glanced back at Cleve. He nodded slowly in acknowledgment of her silent instructions.

"...and then, as soon as her mother had moved in—supposedly to take care of the children—who should show up on the doorstep but her aunt and uncle."

The man standing beside Rachel held a tray of food in one hand and was stuffing his mouth frantically as he spoke. After swallowing the last of some lobster, he set the tray on a table and began to wipe his fingers carefully with a large silk handkerchief. All the while his avid gaze followed the curves of Rachel's body.

Licking the last of the butter from his full, fleshy lips, he murmured, "I believe it's time for dessert." He gave a high-pitched giggle, as though he had said something original and wonderfully clever.

Rachel forced her lips into a provocative smile. "That sounds lovely. There's an alcove just behind us. We could have more privacy there."

"My room is even more private."

She pouted. "If that's really what you want, but..."

"Yes?"

She laughed breathily. "You're going to think I'm a silly old thing."

"No, no," he said eagerly. "Tell me."

"Well...the idea that we're right here in the middle of all these people is, um, very stimulating." She felt heat rise in her face, and she choked a little on the last word, but the man didn't seem to notice.

He wiped his brow with the handkerchief, leaving a sheen of butter. "Yes—yes, I see what you mean."

Sliding his arm around her waist, he held her close as they turned and walked to the alcove. Upon reaching it, Rachel slid onto the padded seat, leaning back against the white satin pillows. When he placed his knee on the seat to join her, she stretched luxuriously.

"I'm so thirsty, darling." She dropped her lashes, her fingers stroking the white satin. "But I'm too comfortable to move." She glanced up at him. "I need something exotic to drink . . . something sensual."

He swallowed heavily, then turned and looked frantically around the room, as though willing a drink to appear, so he wouldn't have to leave. Then, with a regretful glance at her breasts, he shrugged.

"I'll find just the thing for you." He wagged a pudgy finger at her. "You save my place for me."

Rachel laughed appreciatively. Then, when he turned to leave, she glanced around for Cleve. Her brother was slowly making his way toward the alcove, skirting several couples who were dancing.

Suddenly he stopped as though struck, his eyes wide with fear as he gazed at a spot just beyond her.

Snapping her head around, Rachel found herself caught in a liquid gaze. Bruce was standing a foot away from the alcove, observing her carefully.

Flynn walked down the dimly lit hall toward the kitchen, frustration tearing at his nerves. He had just wasted half an hour searching the rooms behind the kitchen. Rooms that had been dug deep into the heart of the mountain. Rooms with locks on the outside.

And still he had found no trace of Rachel. Opening the door that led to the kitchen, he glanced around the huge room. The kitchen staff were still frantically busy preparing food for the party. They hadn't even glanced up when he had crossed the room the first time. He had merely been another man dressed in white and gold.

"Gotcha!"

Jerking his head around, Flynn took in Pete's wide grin. "You don't care much for your teeth, do you?" he said, relaxing slightly. "Haven't you got anything better to do than sneak up behind people?"

Pete shrugged. "I could have stayed with Mrs. Lamont...but I figured you'd never get anything done without me." He shook his head. "That broad belongs in a nuthouse. You wouldn't believe the things she had in mind."

"Tell me about it later," Flynn said. "You haven't seen Rachel, have you?"

Pete shook his head. "I've only had a chance to look back here." He nodded toward the dark hall behind them. "I suppose that's where the permanent residents sleep. It's a little grim, isn't it?"

"They're elegant," Flynn said. "But that doesn't change what they are—slave quarters."

"So what do we do now?"

He inhaled deeply. "We can't do anything until we find Rachel."

He pushed the door open, and the two of them walked across the kitchen and back into the lounge. It seemed even more crowded and noisy than before.

Rachel had to be in this room somewhere, he thought. She had to be.

He had avoided thinking about the possibility that she hadn't been brought to the mansion after all. Because that meant whoever had found her by the stream had disposed of her.

The second he allowed the thought into his head Flynn felt a debilitating weakness attack his limbs and his mind. But he couldn't let that happen. He needed his wits, his strength, if he was going to accomplish anything at all.

Rachel was alive, he told himself roughly. He wouldn't allow it to be any other way. He simply would not allow her to be dead.

"You look sick," Pete said, examining the face of his friend. "What's wrong?"

Flynn shook his head. "Nothing," he said harshly. "I'm fine. And I think I've figured out what to do when we find her. It means you'll have to do a little exploring while I look for her."

As Flynn quietly told Pete his plan, his eyes made another pass around the room. When he suddenly stiffened, Pete stared at him in inquiry. But Flynn wasn't paying attention to his friend. His eyes were trained on a beautiful young woman at the far end of the lounge.

She wore a Grecian gown that barely covered her shapely thighs. It was clasped on one shoulder, then fell in soft white folds across her breasts. The waist was crisscrossed with gold cord, and more of the cord was entwined with her long, blond hair, securing it at the top of her head. On her back was a quiver of golden arrows. She was Diana the huntress; she was Rachel.

Flynn felt emotion surge through him as the ache in his chest disappeared. He examined her face closely for fear or pain. But as she stared up at a gray-haired man her head was held high and proud, and the set of her chin told Flynn she was fighting mad.

He almost laughed, so enveloping was his relief. She was so damn beautiful, so damn gutsy.

"Are you enjoying the party, Sabrina?" Bruce said as his gaze slid over her face.

"Bruce!" she squealed in delight, rising to her knees and laughing gaily. "It's wonderful! Wonderful and wicked and wild." Her body swayed toward him slightly. "I *adore* parties. But this is the party to end all parties. I love it." She reached out to stroke his arm, glancing at him from under her lashes. "I love *everything.*"

His husky laugh sent chills up her spine. "We'll have to explore that thought more thoroughly later, my dear," he said. "Right now I need to see to my other guests. I just wanted to make sure you were enjoying yourself."

When he turned away Rachel slumped back against the pillows. Her heart pounded in her chest, and her stomach churned. What would she do if he really came to her later? But she couldn't think about that. She would just have to make sure she and Cleve got away before the party was over.

Cleve took the last few steps to the alcove and stood beside it, his back to her. "Rachel...my God, *Rachel*. Why did you come? How did you get here?" His voice broke with the last words, and she sensed that he was struggling to pull himself together. "That drug they give us is wearing off...it leaves you depressed." He turned his head to one side. No one but Rachel could see the tormented expression on his face. "Hell, I'll be on a crying jag in a minute." He paused to inhale slowly. "Why, Rachel? For God's sake, why? I've thought of you every day...I wanted to see you so badly. But not like this...not *here*."

"Shh," she said, her voice soothing. "Stop worrying about me. We're going to get out of this mess together." Keeping her eyes on the room, she continued. "I came here with a friend, Cleve. He's still on the outside. If we can just get off the grounds and into the jungle without being seen, we'll have it made."

He slumped back against the wall. "That's impossible. They won't let anyone leave. Do you know how many times I've tried?" He clenched his fists tightly. "They wouldn't even let me kill myself."

"Cleve!" she whispered, her voice shocked. She felt pain shoot through her, but she couldn't give in to it. Not now. Cleve didn't need her sympathy; he needed her strength. "Don't even think of something like that. That's the coward's way, and you're no coward. We'll get out, and you'll be free of this place forever. And when we tell the authorities what's been going on, the people who kept you here will be behind bars for a long time."

It was a long, tense moment before he spoke. "When you say it, I almost believe it's going to happen."

She bit her lip at the longing in his voice. She had to make it happen. Cleve was at the breaking point.

Inhaling deeply, she glanced around the lounge. Her eyes widened and her breath caught in her throat when a man stepped from the shadows on the other side of the lounge. A pirate. A big, bold, gaudy-looking buccaneer.

An explosion of warmth and gladness and love burst in her heart as their eyes met and held for an electrified moment. Flynn had come for her.

In the next few seconds a conversation took place. It was deep and intimate, and it was completely without words. Then, pulling his gaze away from hers, Flynn shot a questioning glance at Cleve. She smiled and nodded.

"Cleve," she said, her voice filled with excitement and renewed strength, "do you see that man across the room? The big man dressed as a pirate . . . wearing indecently tight, white pants?" she added with a disapproving frown.

Her brother followed her gaze, then nodded hesitantly.

"That's the friend I was telling you about. He'll help us, Cleve."

When Pete suddenly appeared beside Flynn, Rachel almost laughed in exhilaration. "And the man beside him in the Roman toga is a friend, too. They'll get us out of here," she said with pride. "The two of them are as good as an army."

Flynn frowned. Rachel's brother had just moved away from the alcove when a grossly obese man joined her. He could almost feel his fingers around the man's throat. But he couldn't join her now without attracting attention. He would have to wait for the plan to go into effect.

Keeping his eyes on the alcove, he said to Pete, "You're sure you've got it all set?"

"Trust me. They won't know what hit 'em." Satisfaction was strong in Pete's voice. "Thirteen seconds to blast off," he said, staring at a crystal wall clock.

They each counted silently, feeling the seconds drag. Then, suddenly, a loud explosion came from the bowels of the mansion. Immediately smoke poured through the doors from the kitchen, filling the lounge. Everywhere people began to scream and shove their neighbors aside in their desperate rush to reach the outer doors.

Flynn moved instantly toward the alcove where he had last seen Rachel. On his way he saw Cleve stumbling over a cowering man. He grabbed the young man's arm and shoved him roughly toward Pete.

"Take him out," he shouted over the noise. "I'll get Rachel and leave right behind you."

Flynn didn't stop to make sure they followed his instructions. Pushing his way through the terrified people, he continued across the room.

The smoke was thick when he finally reached the alcove. The satin-covered cubbyhole was empty. And Rachel was nowhere in sight.

"Rachel!" he shouted, dipping his head against the smoke. "Rachel, where are you?"

Rachel pulled against the fingers that were clasped tightly around her wrist. "We can't go upstairs!" she said, choking on the smoke that surrounded her. "The place is on fire—we've got to get out!"

When the large man ignored her and continued to drag her up the stairs she kicked out at him in frustration. She knew what the fire was. It was Flynn's diversion. It was supposed to be their means of escape. But moments after the explosion the man who had been beside her most of the evening had begun to pull her toward the stairs.

He had to be insane, she thought, struggling wildly to free her hand. No one in his right mind would stay in a burning building.

"Rachel!"

At the sound of her name she swung her head around. It was Flynn. He was on the first level, looking for her. He would never find her if she let this man pull her into his room. As they reached the top of the stairs she fell to her knees on the carpet, jerking her hand sharply.

But he wouldn't let go. As though it was a perfectly normal occurrence, he began to drag her across the floor toward the open door of a bedroom.

"Flynn!" she screamed in fury. "You idiot, you'd better not let me burn. Damn it, get me out of this!"

Having taken the stairs two at a time, Flynn entered the corridor just as the obese man pulled Rachel across the threshold of a bedroom. He rushed forward, feeling an explosion of wrath that almost blinded him. He didn't recognize the animal sound that rose in his throat as he slammed his fist into the man's huge stomach.

In disgust he felt his hand sink into six inches of flaccid flesh. The man bent over, gasping for breath. But it wasn't enough. Flynn wanted to kick him until he bled, until he begged for mercy. But there wasn't time.

Grabbing Rachel's hand, he pulled her to her feet and moved back toward the staircase.

"We can't just leave him!" she shouted. "For God's sake, Flynn. He'll burn."

"Let him burn," he said coldly.

"No," she said, her voice stubborn. "We can't."

Stopping abruptly, he slung her over his shoulder, fireman style, and continued down the stairs. After she had hit him in the back the second time, he said, "Judas Priest, Boston, it was a smoke bomb. No one's going to burn. The smoke will start clearing in a minute."

She stopped struggling. "And Cleve?"

"He's with Pete, on his way to the *Nightingale*. Now can we get the hell out of here?"

At the foot of the stairs he set her on her feet, and they ran. Outside, people were in an uproar, shouting at each other as they tried to find someone to blame. No one even noticed the two people who ran into the jungle.

Flynn made his way by instinct to the stream that would lead them up the side of the mountain. They ran along the bank, jumping over ferns and bushes, every step making their escape more secure.

Suddenly Rachel careened into Flynn's back as he stopped dead in his tracks.

There before them, stepping out of the dark jungle, was the largest man Rachel had ever seen in her life. He was Polynesian and wore a brightly colored *pareu*. Above it the muscles of his bare chest glinted in the moonlight. He didn't have a weapon; he didn't need one. He simply folded his massive arms across his chest and stared at them, as though daring them to take another step.

Starting at the man's bare feet, Flynn ran his gaze up the giant—all seven feet plus of him. "Ohh, hell," Flynn breathed in awe. Then, drawing a deep breath, he threw himself at the man's knees.

"Get to the boat—now!" he called to Rachel.

Rachel glanced at the concealing jungle, then back to the two men. There was no question of her leaving. She knew where she belonged, even if Flynn didn't.

The giant slung Flynn aside as though he were a gnat and took a step toward her. Flynn hit the bushes rolling and was on his feet instantly. With stunning force he slammed his shoulder into the man's lower back, but the man barely swayed. Reaching around, he picked Flynn up and locked him in a crushing bear hug.

Rachel caught her breath when she heard something rip, but it was only the gold shirt. The strain had caused it to split down the front, leaving Flynn's chest bare. Glancing around frantically, she picked up a large fallen branch. Stepping forward, she swung with all her strength, hitting the man in the back of the head. He grunted and shook his head slightly. But he didn't let go of Flynn.

"Damn it, Boston," Flynn wheezed. "You're just annoying him. Get the hell out of here. I've got everything under control."

A short laugh caught in her throat. Nothing could faze Flynn's arrogance. Gritting her teeth, she swung at the giant again.

When the rough club connected with the back of his neck the man staggered backward. Rachel scrambled out of his way, watching in chagrin as, still clutching Flynn, he began to right himself again.

Then luck stepped in. Luck in the form of a jungle vine. The man tripped over it and went sprawling backward, finally loosening his grip on Flynn as he flailed his arms wildly.

Rachel ran to Flynn, who had gone down on his knees when the man let go. "Are you all right?" she asked, clutching his arm anxiously.

"I'm—I'm fine," Flynn gasped. Grabbing her by the neck, he kissed her roughly. "Thanks, Boston."

Unsteadily, he rose to his feet and shook his head. Glancing over his shoulder, he saw the giant untangling his limbs from the trailing vines. "Let's get out of here before he starts ripping up trees."

They didn't stop running until they had crossed the high valley. Even then they didn't stop to rest; they merely slowed down, making their way steadily toward the other side of the island—and freedom.

Throughout the night they walked. For Rachel the dark hours passed in a fog of exhaustion. She had no idea if they were even going in the right direction. She merely followed Flynn.

When she fell to her knees he didn't speak but merely stooped to pick her up in his arms.

"No—" she said weakly. It was the only word she could get out.

"Shut up," he said firmly, cradling her against him as he made his way down the side of the mountain.

The sun was just breaking loose from the eastern horizon when they topped a small rise. Setting her on her feet, Flynn stood and gazed ahead. "Look," he said softly.

Fifty yards below them the *Nightingale* waited in the small secluded bay. Triumph burst in Rachel's chest. Blinking in exhaustion, she saw Cleve and Pete sitting on deck. When they caught sight of Flynn and Rachel, the two men were on their feet instantly, jumping the rail and splashing through the water to meet them.

When at last they were all together on the boat Flynn glanced around at his strange looking crew.

"Let's get under way," he said, the strength returning to his voice.

Pete grinned. "Aye-aye, captain, you old son of a bitch." The enthusiasm and relief in his voice spoke louder than his words. Nimbly he ran to raise the anchor. "Goodbye, Devil's Island. Hello, world!"

Chapter Fourteen

Rachel and Cleve sat on the deck, their arms about each other. They didn't speak. They laughed and they cried, and it was enough for now. Words—explanations—would come to them later, when they weren't so emotional.

After a long while Rachel glanced up and saw Flynn watching them. Her smile was warm and intimate. "I don't think you've ever been formally introduced to my brother. Cleve, this is the captain of the *Nightingale*—Flynn."

After turning his head away briefly to wipe his eyes, Cleve stood and shook Flynn's hand. "I-I don't know how to thank you," he said shyly. "Rachel said you were a friend. You must be a very good one to go through all this."

Flynn shrugged. "She hired me to find you. I did my job."

Although Rachel heard the words it took a moment for the detached, almost cold tone of Flynn's voice to sink in. When it did, she searched his features in confusion. A job? she thought, her mouth going dry. He couldn't mean what he was saying. They both knew it was much more than just a job. Somehow she felt as though he had just slapped her face.

Glancing toward Rachel, but avoiding her eyes, Flynn said, "I just talked to Ralph Terii, a friend in Atuona who's a retired government official. I explained the situation—at least, as much as I could. He said he would make sure there's a plane and men on Iuakea before the smoke clears."

"That's good to hear," Pete called from the cockpit. "I didn't want to think about that fleet of battleships chasing us."

"No one will stop us now," Flynn said, then moved toward the wheel. "I want the three of you to rest now. Especially you, Pete. I'll need you to take over at the wheel in a couple of hours."

Rachel pulled her gaze away from Flynn and reached out to clasp Cleve's hand. "If you want to talk now, I can put off sleeping."

He glanced away, shaking his head in a jerky, negative motion. "I can't," he whispered. "Not now. It's too . . . immediate."

She hugged him close, stroking his face. "I'm here, any time you need to talk. All that matters now is that you're free and we're on our way home."

As she raised her head, her eyes met Flynn's. He stared at her silently for a moment, then, still without speaking, turned his back and took over the wheel.

Pete and Cleve fell asleep immediately, but Rachel tossed and turned restlessly. After an endless hour she sat up on the bunk. She couldn't stop thinking about the strange way Flynn was acting. In the short time they had been together they had experienced a lifetime of events. He couldn't shrug off what was between them so carelessly.

She swung her feet over the side of the bunk and quietly left the cabin. She moved through the darkness to stand beside him at the wheel.

"I thought I told you to rest," he said without looking at her.

"I can't." She gazed out at the ocean for a moment, wondering how to start. No promises had been made verbally; how could she accuse him of breaking a pledge made with a touch, with a look?

Glancing at his stern features, she said hesitantly, "It's hard to believe it's over. It seems like years since we left Atuona. So much has happened. It's been crazy... exciting. In a way it all seems unreal. Then again—" she tried to keep her words from sounding like a plea "—it's somehow more real than anything that's ever happened to me."

For a long time he stared ahead without speaking. "It wasn't." There was no emotion in his voice at all.

The words had an abrupt, dead feel to them. "It was a dream. Now it's time we got back to the real world."

Rachel bit her lip to keep it from trembling. She could feel him shutting her out, but she didn't know what to do about it. "Flynn—"

"Go below and get some sleep." It was an order, short and brusque. The tone was final.

Two days later, after the *Nightingale* slid past Tahuata and Mohotani, they sighted Hiva Oa. Rachel stood on the foredeck, leaning against the mast as she watched the island grow larger and larger.

Flynn had kept in touch with the authorities during the trip back, and they had heard what had happened on Iuakea after their departure. A few of the guests had left on their yachts and, when the authorities caught up with them, had denied all knowledge of the island. But they had caught Bruce as he was boarding his plane. Jean-Paul had disappeared by the time they reached Mana Kula.

The Marquesan authorities were working around the clock trying to sort out the mess. The Pohukaina islanders were back with their people, but the Marquesans still had to take care of the people like Cleve who had been flown in from all over the world and needed transportation back to their homes. It was a tangle that would take weeks to straighten out.

Flynn's friend, Ralph, had sent word that he would be waiting on the dock for them when they arrived, and that he hadn't made up his mind whether he would shake Flynn's hand or punch his face. He sent word that reporters were flying in from all over the world. Atuona would never be the same.

It was satisfying to know that everything had worked out, and Rachel knew she should feel pleased about the part she had played in it. But as she stood on the bow, gazing toward the island of Hiva Oa, the emotion that dominated was a lingering, confused sadness.

Flynn had become more and more distant with each passing hour. Except for those few moments after leaving Iuakca, they hadn't even spoken alone. His emotional desertion left her with an emptiness she had never felt before.

As the *Nightingale* drew near the dock she saw a large group of people waiting for them to arrive. Obviously word had gone out that they were coming in.

One tall man stood separate from the crowd. Rachel blinked rapidly, then, swinging around, she picked up the binoculars. She ran the glasses over the area, then drew in a sharp breath. It was Asa.

The minute the *Nightingale* drew up alongside the dock, Rachel jumped the rail. Her father caught her in his arms and hugged her tightly.

"What are you doing here?" she asked, laughing as she held on to his strong shoulders.

"I've been trying to get in touch with you for a week," he said gruffly. "The only thing I could get out of these people was some nonsense about you disappearing in the middle of the night with a man named Flynn." He frowned down at her. "A man who has a dubious reputation with the authorities. That sounded too crazy even for you, so I flew out here to see what in hell was going on.''

She laughed again. "Oh, Asa, even your scolding sounds good right now. I've got so much to tell you. Wait until you—" She broke off when she saw Cleve walking slowly toward them. "Here comes Cleve." She turned back to her father. "Please be nice to him, Asa. He's had a hard time."

When Cleve reached them, Rachel stepped back. She could see Asa looking Cleve over, sizing him up, but although her father was as gruff as ever, he said nothing to upset the younger man.

Pulling at Asa's hand, she said, "Come on, I want you to meet Flynn and Pete. They saved my life a dozen times in the past week. Pete! Flynn!" she called out.

"This is my father, Asa McNaught," she said when she reached them. "Asa, I want you to meet my friends—Flynn and Pete."

Pete grinned. "Your chin looks good on Rachel, but I'm sure glad she didn't get your build." He reached out and shook hands. "You've got quite a daughter."

"That's what she keeps telling me." Asa smiled, but kept his eyes on Flynn as he spoke.

Flynn shook hands and muttered a brief greeting, then turned back to work on the boat. Rachel felt an intense pain constricting her chest. She might as well have been a stranger to him.

Glancing at her father, she caught him studying her face and forced a smile. "I look a mess," she said, running a hand through her hair. "I think I would give my fox jacket for a real bath and a change of clothes right now.''

"Then let's get moving. Those cracker boxes they call bungalows are too small. A kid named Tea found me a house to rent—now why is that funny?'' Asa asked as Rachel began to laugh. Shaking his head, he glanced toward Cleve. ''There's plenty of room for all of us.''

When Cleve nodded hesitantly, Rachel hugged Asa's arm. She had never known her father could be so sensitive to another person's feelings. Pride filled her as she watched her brother and father walk down the quay together.

Hearing a shout from Pete, she turned and took her bags from him. Once again her eyes sought Flynn, and once again he ignored her completely.

"Come on, girl,'' Asa impatiently called back to her. ''The sooner we get you and the boy rested, the sooner we can get back to civilization.''

"Asa can't stand to wait,'' she said to Pete, smiling hesitantly. ''Well . . . I guess I'll see you later.''

"Not for a while,'' he said. ''I'm leaving for Pohukaina just as soon as I can borrow a boat. I'm going to get Tahia and bring her back to Hiva Oa.''

"Oh, Pete, I'm glad.'' She leaned forward to kiss him. ''You deserve all the happiness in the world.''

Pete smiled, then followed her gaze to the stiffness of Flynn's back. ''I'm sorry,'' he said softly, his eyes full of sympathy.

Rachel raised her chin in an automatic reaction. She didn't want sympathy. She would not be ''poor

Rachel" who fell in love with a wandering man. Swinging around, she walked toward her father and Cleve.

Later that evening, after she had bathed and changed and was standing before an ancient dresser to brush her hair, her father walked into her bedroom.

"Cleve's asleep," he said, answering her question before she could ask it.

"He's slept most of the time since we left the island," she said. "I suppose it's therapeutic."

Asa sat on the bed. "He's a little flaky, but he's not a bad kid."

Rachel raised one brow. That was high praise coming from Asa.

"Now don't get me wrong," he blustered. "I still think he's pretty damn weird . . . but that may be because of the idiot who raised him. He seems bright enough. He just never had an example to follow."

"You mean like I did."

"Exactly," he said in satisfaction, unaware of her teasing smile. "He needs someone to watch him until his brain catches up with his body—someone to guide him until his feet are on solid ground."

"It's a shame you're too busy to take on a job like that," she said, watching him slyly. "Cleve couldn't have a better teacher than you."

"You think so?" He looked up, met her eyes, then laughed in chagrin. "You think you're smart, don't you? As a matter of fact, I've been talking to him about coming to work for me . . . and staying at my place for a while. That damn house is too big for just me—since my only daughter is too independent to live there with me."

"What happened to your wedding plans?"

He smiled wryly. "Paulette figured out that I was using her to keep you home and let me have it good." He paused, frowning. "That made me stop and think about what I was doing. It's been a long time since I've done something I was ashamed of." He glanced at Rachel. "And now that she won't have anything to do with me, I think she's exactly the woman I need."

"Just because you can't have her?"

He shook his head. "No, of course not. Because she's smart and beautiful...and because she was hurt when she found out." He raised his gaze to Rachel. "She really cared for me. It wasn't just my money."

Rachel stooped to hug him. "Don't worry, you'll get her. Hit her with that little boy penitence and she'll fall like a ton of bricks."

She walked back to the mirror to continue brushing her hair. Cleve would grow strong under Asa's care. Her father was gruff and domineering, but he was a good man, a strong man, with strong principles. Cleve would have Asa; Asa would have Cleve and Paulette. Pete had Tahia. Rachel had to fight hard to keep from feeling sorry for herself.

"So you think having the kid come stay with me is a good idea?"

She held the brush still for a moment as she stared at her father's reflection in the mirror. "I think you'll be the father he's always needed...and he'll be the son *you've* always needed."

He stood abruptly, his face shocked. "You're wrong, Rachel. I've never needed a son."

He moved a step in her direction, then stopped and glanced down at the floor in embarrassment. "From the very first minute I saw you," he said, his voice husky with emotion, "I loved you. I couldn't believe that God had given me something as beautiful and wonderful as you." He raised his head to meet her eyes in the mirror. "Why do you think I fought your mother so hard to keep you? If I had had a dozen sons, I couldn't have been prouder or loved them more."

Rachel felt tears sting her eyes. She turned and walked into his arms. After a few seconds he shook her off. "That's enough of that," he said gruffly. "When will you be ready to leave?"

She stared down at her hands.

"Rachel?"

Glancing up, she smiled. "I'm not going, Asa. I'm going to stay on Hiva Oa."

"Well, hell, girl, how long a vacation do you need?" The words were belligerent, but his eyes were sharp with concern as he watched her.

She drew in a deep breath. "It's not a vacation. I'm going to live here."

"That's crazy. You stop this nonsense and come home where you belong." When she didn't respond he said stiffly, "It's that man Flynn, isn't it?"

"Partly," she admitted. "But even if I hadn't found Flynn, I would stay. You see, I fell in love with the people and the islands. Asa, it's a completely different world. There's nothing artificial here. They don't try to complicate life. It's strange and beautiful—a way of life I never even dreamed existed. Sometimes it's hard, but it's always real." She shrugged, finding words inadequate. "I just know this is where I belong."

He shook his head vigorously, as though trying to deny what he was hearing. "That's just a lot of fancy talk. You're staying because you've got a yen for that no-account adventurer." He shook his head. "You'd abandon all you've worked for... the complex... for a beach bum? Damn it, Rachel, where's your pride? The man obviously doesn't want you." He frowned suddenly. "Who in hell does he think he is, anyway? Rejecting Asa McNaught's daughter."

She laughed in genuine amusement. "I guess he didn't know you would take it as a personal insult."

Slowly, he examined her features. "You really love him, don't you?"

She shrugged. "I'm afraid so."

"I don't like seeing you unhappy," he grumbled. "Do you want me to buy him for you?"

She laughed. The suggestion was typical of Asa. He would use every means at his disposal to make things right for her. For a second, just a flash of time, she wished that Flynn were the kind of man who could be bought. But only for a moment. If he could be bought, then he wouldn't be Flynn, and she wouldn't love him so desperately.

Chapter Fifteen

Two days later Rachel watched Asa and Cleve leave on the plane that would take them to Nuku Hiva, then to Tahiti, then to the States. She smiled and waved at Cleve, who stared down at her from the window seat.

Her brother was still unsure of himself, and of the future. He hadn't wanted to leave Rachel, but there were too many bad memories for him in this part of the world. Rachel knew that under Asa's brusque care and wise guidance Cleve would grow to be a strong man. And maybe someday he would be able to visit her here, in her new home, without being haunted by the nightmares of his stay on Bruce's Devil's Island.

It was only as the plane disappeared from sight that she remembered today was Cleve's birthday. It seemed a sign somehow. A beginning for both of them.

Turning her back on the landing strip, she began to walk away. It was time for her to get on with her own part of the future.

An hour later she turned the corner onto Pigalle. She carried both her suitcases, and her chin was high as she walked toward Fauzy's. She was pushing her way through a crowd of people who had gathered around a cockfight when she saw Flynn.

She stared at his face for a moment. He obviously wasn't enjoying himself. The islanders were yelling enthusiastically, urging the birds on, but Flynn stood with his hands in his pockets, the aloofness of his features separating him from the crowd.

Making her way around the circle, she approached him from behind. "Hello, Flynn," she said quietly.

His shoulders stiffened; then he slowly turned to face her. For a few seconds he merely stared at her, then he glanced back at the cockfight. "I figured you had already left."

She examined the harsh lines of his face, her heart aching at the unhappiness she saw there. "You're lying, Flynn. You knew I wouldn't leave with Asa and Cleve." She paused. "We have some unfinished business."

He shook his head. "You can forget the five hundred . . . we'll call the debt paid."

"I'm not talking about the money. The unfinished business I'm talking about is what's between us."

He turned back to her, meeting her steady gaze. "There's nothing between us. We had a fling. Big deal." He shrugged carelessly. "I admit it was fun. I've never made it with a socialite before, and I believe in broadening my range of experience...but now it's over."

She held his gaze for long, silent moments. "It will never be over," she said, the words low and intense.

He moved his shoulders as though they ached, and expelled a heavy breath. "Damn it, I hate clinging women!" he said explosively. "You give them a roll in the hay and they think they own you." Laughing harshly, he turned and began to push his way through the people around them. "Believe me," he said over his shoulder, "whatever you feel, you'll get over it. But do it without bothering me."

"Don't you dare walk away from me!" she warned in fury, following him to the edge of the crowd. "We're going to get this settled, Flynn. Come back here!"

He kept walking. "I'm a loner, Boston," he shouted. "I don't need anyone but myself."

Raising her chin, she shouted to his retreating back, "You need *me*! Damn it, Flynn, *you need me*!"

For a mere second he paused, then, without glancing back, he continued to walk away.

Hours later, as she sat in the chair beside the bed in the same room she had had before, Rachel frowned into the darkness. She wouldn't let him defeat her. She would stick to him like a burr. Sooner or later he would have to admit they belonged together. He had to, she told herself, clenching her fists.

She turned her head slowly when she heard laughter in the hall, then a low voice. Flynn. Moving silently, she eased the door open just a crack and looked into the dimly lit hall.

He was standing in front of his door, fitting the key into the lock. And the Japanese woman Rachel had seen on her first day in Atuona was clinging to his arm.

As though sensing her presence, Flynn glanced over his shoulder. He stared at her for a moment, then, still holding her gaze, he opened the door of his room and ushered the woman inside.

Rachel closed the door slowly. She bit her lip sharply when it began to quiver. She wouldn't let him get to her. The whole scene had been staged for her benefit, but it wouldn't work. He could sleep with every woman in the South Pacific, and Rachel would still know that they belonged together.

"You stubborn bastard," she whispered to the darkness as she resumed her place by the bed. "I hope you're impotent."

Closing the door, Flynn flicked on the light and looked down at the woman beside him.

"We all missed you, Flynn," she said, laughing. "The town was too tame, too dull, while you were gone."

She wrapped her slender arms around his neck and kissed him deeply. Flynn waited for the old familiar feeling to hit him—he waited for a long time—but nothing happened. Holding Bella tighter, he slid his hands down her back. And still nothing happened.

Swearing in frustration, he turned his back on her.

"Hey, Flynn," she said gently. "You're just tense. Come lie down on the bed and let Bella give you a massage. Guaranteed to work."

He drew a deep breath and turned around to face her. "Not tonight, Bella. I think I need some sleep." Reaching into his pocket, he pulled out a twenty-dollar bill. "Thanks anyway."

"Hey, you don't owe me anything. You think I'm a charity case or something? I earn my money."

"Please," he said quietly. "Call it a gift. Go out and buy yourself something pretty."

She hesitated, then shrugged and took the money. At the door, she looked over her shoulder. "You got problems, Flynn?"

He laughed harshly. "I got problems, Bella. But I guess I'll have to work them out some other way."

When she had gone Flynn began to pace. What in hell had Rachel done to him? Damn it, why did she have to come here in the first place? He had been doing all right without her.

He stopped pacing and leaned his head back wearily. It was a lie. He hadn't been all right. He had never been all right until he met Rachel.

He tried to replace Rachel's image with the gentle, loving face of Lili. But it was useless. He couldn't even remember what Lili had looked like. The loss saddened him momentarily. Lili had never exasperated him. She had never goaded him until he exploded. Lili had never set him on fire.

Leaning against the door, he closed his eyes. He had known on Iuakea that he loved Rachel, and he had spent the time since then fighting it. But damn it to hell, he didn't want to be in love. Rachel might seem to be all that was good and bright, but she could hurt him. She could hurt him as he had never been hurt before. All he could do now was figure out if loving her was worth taking that chance.

Rachel stared straight ahead into the darkness. Her mind was full of pictures. Pictures of Flynn and the woman he had taken to his room. Why did she have to have such a vivid imagination?

Jerking her head up, she listened as a key was inserted into the lock. The door opened slowly, and Flynn stepped into the room. He closed the door behind him and simply stood there for a while without speaking. Then he moved further into the room.

When he was right in front of her, he stopped. She could feel his eyes on her face. "I hate golf," he said abruptly.

She swallowed heavily. "Yes, I know," she whispered.

"And I hate Wall Street."

"Flynn, I wouldn't ask you to go back there."

"But you can't stay here. It's not your world. The Marquesans don't need any shopping malls."

"No," she said slowly. "But maybe they need someone tough enough and savvy enough to keep away the malls and the condos."

Leaning his head back, he closed his eyes. "All I've got is the *Nightingale*. It's my home," he said, his voice so tight it hurt her to hear it. "I can't offer mansions, or expensive clothes, or fancy parties."

"I don't need any of those things." Her hands clenched and unclenched. "Can't the *Nightingale* be my home, too?"

Silence fell again. The tension in the room was palpable. She waited…and waited until she could take no more.

"Say it, Flynn." She almost moaned the words. "Just say it."

He took one step and jerked her up into his arms, holding her as if he would never let her go. "I need you, Rachel," he whispered harshly against her neck. "*God*, I need you."

Rachel met his seeking lips. Now they both knew they belonged together.

Take 4 Silhouette Intimate Moments novels
FREE

Then preview 4 brand new Silhouette Intimate Moments® novels —delivered to your door every month—for 15 days as soon as they are published. When you decide to keep them, you pay just $2.25 each ($2.50 each, in Canada), *with no shipping, handling, or other charges of any kind!*

Silhouette Intimate Moments novels are not for everyone. They were created to give you a more detailed, more exciting reading experience, filled with romantic fantasy, intense sensuality, and stirring passion.

The first 4 Silhouette Intimate Moments novels are absolutely FREE and without obligation, yours to keep. You can cancel at any time.

You'll also receive a FREE subscription to the Silhouette Books Newsletter as long as you remain a member. Each issue is filled with news on upcoming titles, interviews with your favorite authors, even their favorite recipes.

To get your 4 FREE books, fill out and mail the coupon today!

◐ *Silhouette Intimate Moments*®

Silhouette Books, 120 Brighton Rd., P.O. Box 5084, Clifton, NJ 07015-5084

Silhouette Special Edition

COMING NEXT MONTH

#385 FORBIDDEN FRUIT—Brooke Hastings
Noble Lady Georgina felt obliged to marry her social equal. But
when her grandmother hired macho, working-class Mike Napoli to
chaperone Georgina, attraction soon outranked obligation!

#386 MANDREGO—Tracy Sinclair
Elissa had vowed to avenge her father's ruin. Her plot led her to
an island paradise—and into the arms of her enemy's bodyguard,
dangerously attractive Troy Benedict. Could revenge possibly be so
sweet?

#387 THE MIDNIGHT HOUR—Jude O'Neill
Sassy Cleo and wise-cracking Gus were once partners in mystery
writing and marriage, but their famed collaboration had led to
calamity. If they reunited, would they be crafty enough to write
themselves a happy ending?

#388 THE BABY TRAP—Carole Halston
Ginny Sutherland wanted a baby—without the complication of
remarrying. Still, she'd need a male temporarily, and virile Ed
Granger might just be the man for the job....

#389 THE SUN ALWAYS RISES—Judith Daniels
Restaurateur Catherine Harrington didn't want to love and lose
again, but wandering, "no-commitments" Nick O'Donovan was
convincing her to take the risk....

#390 THE FAIRY TALE GIRL—Ann Major
When her fairy tale marriage failed, Amber Johnson left the
Bahamas with her illusions destroyed. So how could she believe
rancher Jake Kassidy's promise that with him she'd live happily
ever after?

AVAILABLE THIS MONTH:

**#379 VOYAGE OF THE
NIGHTINGALE**
Billie Green

#380 SHADOW OF DOUBT
Caitlin Cross

#381 THE STAR SEEKER
Maggi Charles

#382 IN THE NAME OF LOVE
Paula Hamilton

**#383 COME PRIDE, COME
PASSION**
Jennifer West

#384 A TIME TO KEEP
Curtiss Ann Matlock

ATTRACTIVE, SPACE SAVING BOOK RACK

Display your most prized novels on this handsome and sturdy book rack. The hand-rubbed walnut finish will blend into your library decor with quiet elegance, providing a practical organizer for your favorite hard-or soft-covered books.

Only $9.95

Approximately 16" x 8" when assembled

Assembles in seconds!

To order, rush your name, address and zip code, along with a check or money order for $10.70* ($9.95 plus 75¢ postage and handling) payable to *Silhouette Books.*

Silhouette Books
Book Rack Offer
901 Fuhrmann Blvd.
P.O. Box 1325
Buffalo, NY 14269-1325

Offer not available in Canada.

* New York residents add appropriate sales tax.

BKR-2R

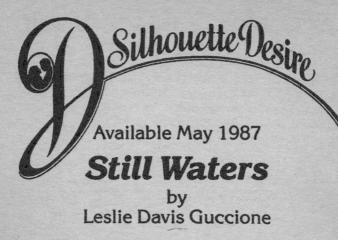

Silhouette Desire

Available May 1987

Still Waters

by
Leslie Davis Guccione

If Drew Branigan's six feet of Irish charm won you over in *Bittersweet Harvest*, Silhouette Desire #311, there's more where he came from—meet his hoodlum-turned-cop younger brother, Ryan.

In *Still Waters*, Ryan Branigan gets a second chance to win his childhood sweetheart, Sky, and this time it's for keeps.

Then look for *Something in Common*, coming in September, 1987, and watch the oldest Branigan find the lady of his dreams.

After raising his five younger brothers, confirmed bachelor Kevin Branigan had finally found some peace. He certainly didn't expect vibrant Erin O'Connor to turn his world upside down!

D353-1